SIX

THE DECLARATION

A SIX THRILLER

J.M. MANYANGA

Big Brains
PUBLISHING LLC

Published by Big Brains Publishing LLC
www.bigbrainspublishing.com

First Edition, December 2023
Paperback ISBN: 978-1-7367883-8-7
e-Book ISBN: 978-1-7367883-7-0

Publisher's Cataloging-in-Publication
(Provided by Cassidy Cataloguing Services, Inc.)

Names: Manyanga, J. M., author.
Title: The declaration : a SIX thriller / J. M. Manyanga.
Description: First edition. | [Saint Louis, Missouri] : Big Brains Publishing LLC, [2023] | Series: SIX series ; book 2.
Identifiers: ISBN: 978-1-7367883-8-7 (paperback) | 978-1-7367883-7-0 (e-Book) | 978-1-7367883-9-4 (audiobook) | LCCN: 2023924240
Subjects: LCSH: Diplomatic documents--Fiction. | Espionage--Fiction. | Spies--Fiction. | International crimes--Fiction. | Africa--Fiction. | LCGFT: Thrillers (Fiction) | Detective and mystery fiction. | Action and adventure fiction. | BISAC: FICTION / Mystery & Detective / International Crime & Mystery. | FICTION / Thrillers / Espionage. | FICTION / Thrillers / Crime. | FICTION / Thrillers / General. | FICTION / Crime.
Classification: LCC: PS3613.A5858 S592 2023 | DDC: 813.6--dc23

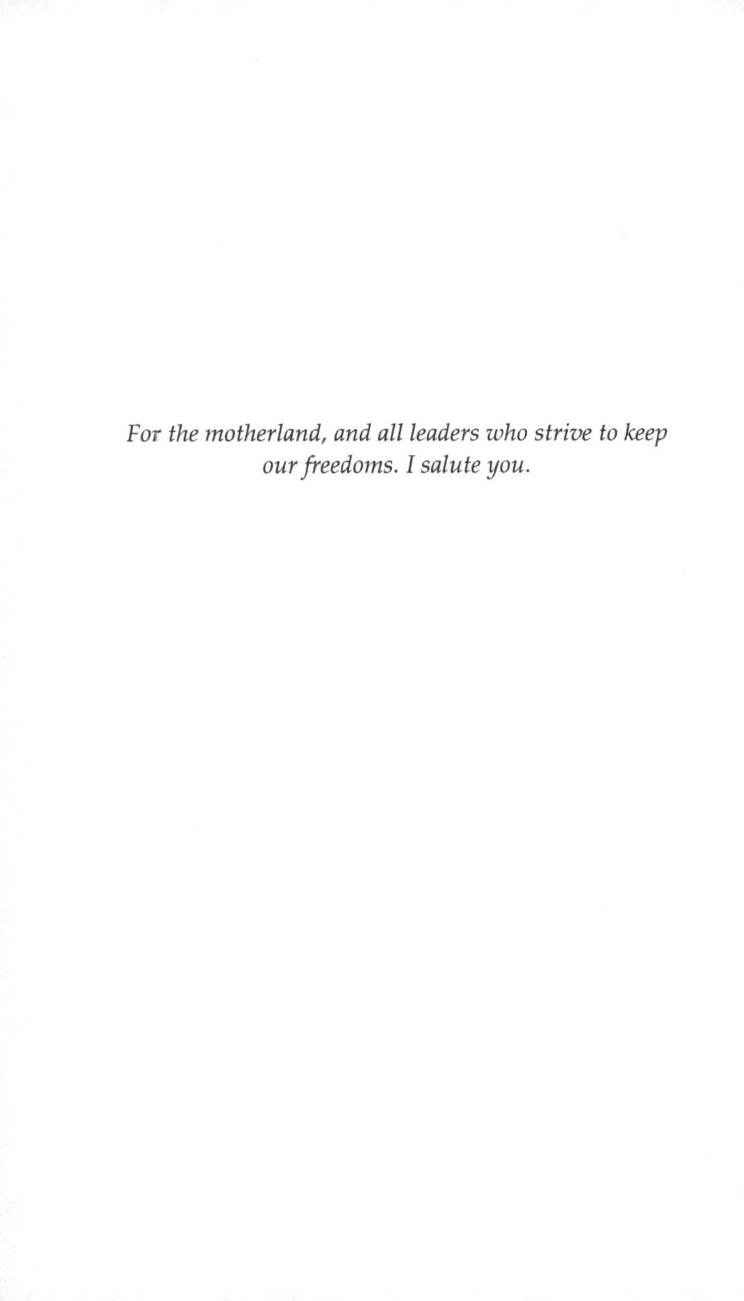

For the motherland, and all leaders who strive to keep our freedoms. I salute you.

ACKNOWLEDGMENTS

I'm grateful for the continued support from my family and friends; I couldn't have written this book without them.

Super thanks to countless people who continue to inspire me every day, intentionally or by chance.

THE DECLARATION

CHAPTER
ONE

THE MAN GAGGED, gasping for air. Any muffled sounds were covered by the blaring TV. The victim kicked, scratched, twitched, and turned. The iron arms pressed the pillow against his face. The victim sank his nails into his attacker's coat-protected arms. Those arms did not budge. His attacker felt the adrenaline rushing through his veins. Squeezing life out of his victim. Such power. Nothing like it. Ah! Every time. What was his victim's crime? He didn't care. He only followed orders.

The man twitched two more times, then his body gave one last violent shudder, and it all stopped. His legs went limp, and the man's grip relaxed, and his arms loosened beside him. The intruder removed the pillow and checked for a pulse. He neatly covered the body with the ornamented linen and silk bed sheets. Oriental. Rich. *Whoever the man was, he must have been important. Or whatever he had in the safe.* He closed his victim's wide-open bloodshot eyes. He wiped tiny droplets of sweat from his own forehead. He stood over the body for a few more seconds to make sure he was dead. Satisfied, he gulped the whiskey on the nightstand without the glass touching his lips. He sat at the edge of the bed. It took him a few moments to get back down to earth. He checked the dead victim again and staggered into the bathroom. After taking off his leather gloves, he washed his face, momentarily marveling at the 24-karat-gold-plated sink faucet and thick white Calacatta marble countertop. *Must cost a fortune,* he thought. He dabbed his face dry with the toilet paper which he flushed down the toilet. He straightened his glasses in the bathroom mirror.

After making sure all the contents of the man's safe were in his briefcase, he exited the suite into an empty hallway, clipping the "Do Not Disturb" sign outside the door. *How long is it going to take you to find out?* The hallway was deserted towards the elevator. A good thing for him. His own room was on the third floor, one of the two rooms he had reserved in hotels adjacent to each other. Both under different names. Paid in cash. Not as big and expensive as the suite he had just left. But it did just fine by him. Fancy room service, and the most comfortable bed he had had in a while. It provided for some much-needed sleep, which he hardly got when on missions. He locked the door behind himself and set the briefcase on the nightstand, then placed his gun above it. You could never be too careful.

The man sat at the edge of his bed for ten minutes, breathing deeply through his diaphragm. At 9:40 p.m., he left the room and used the stairs down to the second floor, avoiding the motion camera above the doorway to the stairway. He paused, then walked briskly into the elevator with a group of elegantly dressed patrons headed down for dinner. He nodded at them, smiled, and looked away. He left the elevator along with the group, avoiding another camera on the ceiling. The lobby area was crowded. He squeezed his way through the crowd out onto the stone-cobbled pavement between buildings into the beautiful Moroccan night.

He retrieved the burner phone from his pocket and pressed the speed dial. A female voice replied.

"Is it done?"

"It's done!"

"Well done," the voice said. "The carrier will pick it up shortly."

"Got it. And the money?"

"The rest of it is coming to you right now."

He paused a few minutes while checking his other phone. A notification popped up on that phone. Two million dollars into his offshore account.

"Received!" he said, satisfied.

In a second that money trail would disappear and become so convoluted that even the FBI or MI6 could not track it. As if the transaction never happened.

"Pleasure doing business with you. I will be in touch."

The man did not answer. He only hung up.

———

AFTER THE CALL, he walked back upstairs and packed his items into his duffel bag and left the room for the one across the street. He didn't trust anyone. Especially whoever was being sent to collect the safe's contents. Certainly not his clients. He knew they could be watching him. It was the "Hunter being the hunted" type of situation. That's how it usually worked in his world, a dog-eat-dog world. His high-profile clients always had several backup plans to tie up loose ends or eliminate incompetence if first-line plans went south. They had more to lose. You kill or you get killed. Those were the rules of the game. He remembered the many times he had narrowly survived being targeted by his clients. That was his world. Seemed like even the rich sometimes wanted their dirty deeds done for free. You help kill their target; they hunt you to get their money back.

From the hotel across the street, he had been observing his target at the Royal Tulip City Center hotel for the previous three days. The streets were jostling with people, mainly teenagers, late on a Saturday night. He joined the crowds, then took a left a few blocks down before veering back on the other side of the building. The other hotel had two entrances, and he used the one facing the ocean. And took stairs to his room. From its window, he waited and spied through the small binoculars.

Ten minutes passed. Then he saw a woman dressed as a hotel housekeeping staffer approach his other room, pushing a serving trolley.

He read her lips. "Room service," she said.

The woman unlocked the door and went inside. The rest of the room was obstructed from his view. He waited. Moments later, he noticed her walk out and push the trolley down the hallway to the elevator as the fire alarm went off. The man watched for a few more minutes. There were no more people. He sat on the bed, gulped a few vials of sleeping pills and took off his shoes as sleep overcame him. His mind was okay. The pills helped.

Hardly an hour later he was woken up by another phone call.

"Did you secure the document?" the gravelly voice from the other end said.

"Yes, sir. I delivered the contents as agreed."

"Dammit! Our source was wrong. Those papers were nothing! You got nothing! I want that document. You hear me? I want that document before Sunday next week! Don't fail me again!"

"Understood! I won't fail you again, Father."

The caller slammed down the phone. If the mission succeeded, he would become a much richer man. If not—

Karim placed his gun next to his pillow. He went back to sleep.

CHAPTER
TWO

THE AIR TEMPERATURE had dropped drastically, welcoming the beginning of winter. Chris thought May was too early for chilly weather.

"Welcome, Mr. Osage," said the restaurant host, calling Chris by name and taking his sport coat. Chris chose the table nearest the rear of the restaurant. Bossa nova music played in the background. The pumpkin-spice-scented candles burning on each table completed the fine-dining ambiance.

Chris was always punctual. He had arrived fifteen minutes before the reserved time. This was his favorite restaurant in town—one of Cape Town's only two Michelin-starred restaurants. His wife and daughter's favorite too. A fusion of Southern European and Mediterranean, with local produce and fresh catch from the nearby Atlantic and Indian oceans. The menu evolved with the seasons. They liked the wine selection here too. Often it required reservations made no less than three months in advance, but he had made this reservation at the last minute with just a phone call. A perk for being a good, well-known regular. Could get anywhere with one phone call.

He checked his watch. His wife Sheila and daughter Colette should be arriving anytime now. A message beeped on his phone. It read: *On our way* It was from Colette. He locked his phone, exposing the wallpaper image of his family—himself, Sheila, and Colette. She was always late—like her mother. Teenagers! *A woman thing,* he thought. It was the makeup. His wife always said she felt uncomfortable without it. And now Colette was at that age where she used it. But Chris didn't mind at all. Being the spouse of a high-profile figure required a level of elegance, because you never knew when the paparazzi would be aiming at you. Sheila preserved that image and reputation well. Chris was proud that she was his wife. He shook his head, reminding himself this was a misogynistic topic to think about.

Colette had been looking forward to this evening, and he had promised her he would be there to celebrate before she started a new year of high school. His wife wanted him to be there. He was a busy man, but he also knew he had to be there for their daughter. Both Sheila and Colette had agreed to meet him. He wanted to be an example of how a man treats a woman, rather than have schools, the government, popular culture, the media, or some other douchebag, indoctrinate her and show her how to be loved.

He had been a lucky man to marry Sheila. A jackpot, as he would tell his golf buddies. She was a traditional woman who enjoyed being a wife and mother. Kind, generous, feminine, and wanted to change the world for better ever since they met.

She loved being a woman. From a good family. That had made his life easier to provide for them and others. She had always been his rock, believing in him when he had nothing. Been with him through thick and thin. She had stood by him, and supported his lead, even back when all he had was dreams and aspirations. She was his rock. She was his queen. He knew she should have much credit for their fortune and helping build their empire. And now all they wanted was to contribute to strengthening their family's legacy, which his parents and his ancestors had not had an opportunity to do.

A minute later, he watched as his wife and daughter made a beeline for the table and was awestruck by the resemblance. At sixteen, Colette looked almost exactly like her mother, except her nose, which came from him. That was a good thing. He kissed his wife, then his daughter, and drew out chairs for them. His bodyguards knew enough to let him do that.

"You both look gorgeous!" Chris said.

"Thanks, honey!"

"Thanks, Dad!"

Sheila held his hand across the table while a server took her coat.

"Sorry, honey. Traffic was unusually dense this evening," Sheila said.

"It's alright. Only a few minutes after eight." He smiled at his daughter.

"It's the rugby sevens championship," Colette said. "The Springboks are playing the All Blacks."

"That makes sense."

"I'm famished!" Colette said, biting into the

Italian garlic bread on the saucer, and perusing the ten-course dinner menu.

"Me too." Chris motioned to the server.

The server brought appetizers.

"Everything okay, honey?" Sheila said.

"Yes. Everything is fine." He smiled. Sheila gazed at him and smiled. She knew him well, and that there were some aspects of his work that could not be discussed with her. Nonetheless she trusted his decisions to be right. She had always done so, and he had not let her down. He was a great man.

"Excited to celebrate my little princess turning sixteen."

Colette blushed. "Daaad! I'm not a kid anymore."

The trio laughed.

"You'll always be daddy's little princess."

Colette rolled her eyes at her father.

"Okay, Princess. What's the big news for your birthday?"

Sheila said, "Colette wants to take her friends to Zanzibar, across several monuments. To learn the history of the continent."

"Really? That sounds like a fun trip—and complex. Who is doing the planning?"

"I am," Colette said. "Mom is helping too. We want to visit all the places we have been learning about in our African history class."

"That's awesome," Chris said. "When is this?"

"This Tuesday."

Chris was about to say something when Sheila squeezed his hand and their eyes locked. He loved that about her. This was a sign for him to tone it down.

Chris looked at his daughter. "I'm happy for

you, honey. Can you send the itinerary to Joel once completed?"

"I will."

"That's going to be expensive."

"I saved all my allowance and dog-walking money this semester. You said you will match whatever I save, remember?"

"I said that, didn't I?"

"Yes, you did."

"Okay." Chris smiled. She reminded him of his younger self.

"I know it's expensive," she said. "But we can take trains to travel between some countries or use public transport. That way we can learn the local cultures."

Chris looked at his wife, then back to his daughter.

"How many of you are going?"

"Four."

"That's dangerous."

"No one knows us. I watched videos of other students trekking and backpacking across Africa and they were fine. I've been telling you for over a month now."

"Oh, yes." Chris took a breath and looked at his wife, who nodded.

"That is true, honey. She has been trying to have you look at the papers for a while now."

"I'm sorry, princess. I know. I have been so busy lately." Chris took and held his daughter's hand.

"How long is the trip?"

"Two weeks."

"Let me think about it."

"Please. I will FaceTime you every day, and you

can track where we are. Live tracking all the time. All our tours will be guided, and we have guides in every spot. And I'll be back in time for the internship at your office."

"Joel and Luis will go with you."

"That's fine. But please can you tell them to lose the suits and ties. That will be embarrassing." Joel and Luis were Colette's bodyguards.

Colette retrieved a pile of stapled papers and slid them on the table. She wanted to have the papers now. Her efforts to leave the papers on his home office desk had not succeeded.

"That's the complete itinerary," she said.

"You're not going to be posting this trip on social media, are you?"

"Not during the trip. We will afterward. Do you know how long it takes to edit the footage and pictures and make clean videos? To get the ones with just the right poses?"

"A lot, I bet."

"A lot."

Chris skimmed through the papers. The itinerary was detailed. Like her mother, Colette was very meticulous, sometimes overly meticulous. But that was good. Chris was worried, but seeing the joy on their daughter's face and the amount of work and discipline she had put in, he knew he could not refuse. A little risk and adventure were healthy. That experience might be handy in the future when she took over the empire.

MOMENTS LATER, Chris shoved a man who

had approached their table, before Chris's protective detail dragged the journalist away.

This often happened in public. As a billionaire, he was vigilant at all times. He wanted to be sure people loved him for himself rather than for what he could provide. Many envied him and a few respected him. A man with practically enough resources to get whatever he wanted. Now the fate of a continent depended on him. He shook the thought away.

Chris sipped the Tokara red wine and turned to his wife, who was unfazed. She was used to hecklers.

"How's the gala prep going?" he asked.

"Everything is on schedule," Sheila said. "We hope to raise enough money to build another dormitory."

"I know you will."

"I appreciate that." Chris kissed his wife. They enjoyed their meals.

"Who's ready for some dessert?" Chris said, lifting the glass bell from the chocolate cake that had been just brought to the table. White smoke wafted out from beneath the glass. Colette was delighted.

Moments like these were sparse: Just himself, his wife, and his daughter alone, in peace. That's what you lost when you became very successful. With the money came a whole load of extra responsibilities, one of which was becoming a public figure. So he cherished these little moments where the three of them could sit down, chat, and eat. Usually this would be followed by a movie either Sheila or Colette picked. He liked most of their choices.

Colette was his pride—an only child. They had wanted a second child, which Chris always hoped would be a son, but the biological clock had other plans. They had tried all avenues: natural, diet, holistic, prayers, IVF. Nothing had worked. He loved Colette and knew the weight was on her as the sole heir to their empire and their legacy. He liked that she enjoyed going with him to the office sometimes. And he tried to teach her as much as he could for her age. They tried not to spoil her and let her earn money by doing chores at the house.

At fifty, Chris looked a decade younger. Chiseled. Ripped. Sharp. Heck, he could bench-press 150 pounds, more than he could in his twenties. Felt in better shape than he had ever been. Few signs of a dad bod. He felt stronger and more in control than he had ever been for a body that had survived years of working 80 to 100 hours a week, on three hours' sleep, and panic attacks, since he began building his business empire in his mid-twenties. His motto had always been to outlast his competitors. Hence health was a priority. Unlimited resources, clean food, and personal trainers for both the body and mind made it possible, with occasional testosterone-boosting injections. This kept him invigorated in his busy schedule. Plus having Sheila by his side made life easier. He knew she deserved everything they had.

CHAPTER
THREE

OPHÉLIE WAITED at the Royal Tulip hotel and watched her target leave the hotel bar and go up the stairs. She spoke in French to the bartender.

The Tangier hotel oozed upper-class style from the moment she had entered. Golden frescoes lining the hotel lobby, purple upholstery and drapery, in imitation of royalty, and expensive. Not flamboyant, but lush—wealthy lush. All the colors, relics, artifacts, art, and materials had been carefully chosen. The marble walls, mahogany floors, paintings and sculptures, the exposed wooden beams along the ceiling. Ophélie concluded that decorating this space alone had cost in the millions.

She checked the clock hanging on the wall above the glass cabinet: 9:35 p.m. He should be coming down any minute now for their meeting. She had seen him come in half an hour ago. In five minutes, she could pay him a visit. She wondered what he was doing right now. Probably drinking wine and keeping an eye on local news. She finished her glass of Sauvignon Blanc. The bartender asked if she wanted another one, and she declined. The hotel restaurant only had a few patrons, sparsely seated across the room. She had chosen a seat at the bar, since she was alone. She wore a rose-colored dress, lilac earrings, and high heels.

She checked the clock again. All she needed was in her tiny clutch bag, containing all items needed to get the job done. Four more minutes. She guzzled the remaining wine and sipped on the water.

She walked to the elevator as several people were coming out. A man got off last. The man triggered an instinct in her. An instinct. Maybe his face. A cold expression. Maybe his heavy mustache that seemed set askew. His glasses. She ignored the feeling and headed to the room. Her line of work had helped her develop a sixth sense for whatever seemed out of place. There was something unusual about that guy.

The first sign was that the door was not locked. She slowly opened the door. The man was lying peacefully face-up on the bed. The closet was open, and the safe open. After making sure there was no one in the room, she tiptoed to the bed and checked his pulse. None. Dead. She retrieved the pocketknife from her purse. She grabbed the remote control from the bedside table and lowered the TV's volume. She waited and listened. There were no sounds. She approached the closed bathroom door and listened. No sounds but the toilet reservoir still filling up from its most recent use, within the last minute or so. She swung the bathroom door open. There was no one. She rushed to the window and opened the curtain. She saw the man with the mustache and glasses about to disappear into the alley. He looked up to that exact window and their eyes locked. He quickly looked away.

―――――――

OPHÉLIE, a former French intelligence agent, was now a private contractor. She was used to death, having been born in Eritrea into a poverty-stricken family. Her family had emigrated to France when she was four, escaping a ten-year civil war caused by a coup by the army's general. Growing up in an immigrant ghetto in the south of France was tough. Her father used to do piece jobs while her mother cleaned houses to make ends meet for the family of eight. Her father died from snorting heroin blended with fentanyl. The agency had found her then. From early on she had learned that to survive she had to fend for herself by what-ever means was necessary. The rough upbringing had taught her self-reliance.

At sixteen she was recruited by the French in-telligence services for their African operation. She agreed. The pay was good, and she could help her siblings. She also saw this as a chance to lead French intelligence operations in Africa, particu-larly central and west Africa. A way to help her homeland. She also hated the rich politicians who stole resources from the people they had sworn to serve. She had seen first-hand how corruption had ruined her country, resulting in unnecessary civil wars, strife, and rampant assassinations of political leaders. How that had torn her family apart, and left her with only vague memories of childhood.

Part of her knew that what she did was wrong, but a larger part of her saw this as a necessary evil.

She dialed a number from her contacts.

"He is dead! Someone else got here before I got to him."

"Did you talk to him?" the voice on the other end said.

"No. He was already dead."

"Someone is watching us. Be careful."

"Okay."

Ophélie exited the room, past a hotel house-keeper who had just emerged from the elevator pushing a serving cart. They both smiled at each other. To avoid the camera, Ophélie used the stairs down. Then she pulled a fire alarm lever. She joined the commotion in the lobby as security tried calming everyone, saying it was a false alarm. She left the hotel and walked down the busy sidewalk. She knew someone might be doing surveillance. *Who was the man in glasses?* A block later, she ditched the mob and found a place to change her clothes. She reached her prefab cottage fifteen minutes later.

CHAPTER
FOUR

SIX HAD ALREADY DRIVEN for seven hours from Zimbabwe's capital, Harare. At each of three roadblocks he had been flagged down and then signaled to proceed when he had almost slowed down to a complete stop. Six found this frustrating. He realized that the police were looking for expired car registrations placed on the left side of the front windshield. Six had tried to maintain the speed limit wherever he could see the road signs. The poor road conditions and potholes in unexpected areas ensured drivers drove more slowly, anyway.

A large portion of the road was under construction, and he took a detour, using a gravel road for almost two hours in the searing heat. The small white Toyota sedan had held its own off-road, but was now covered in red dust.

The fourth roadblock appeared at the turnoff towards Beitbridge. Roadblocks were frequent here to deter illegal diamond traders and illegal artisanal small-scale mining from newly discovered diamond mines. The government now patrolled the whole area, but illegal small-scale miners remained a problem. The place hadn't changed since the last time he had been here, except for deeper and more dangerous potholes, which doubled Six's estimated time of arrival. He watched as several cars in front of him were stopped and let go, while others were simply flagged down and signaled to proceed without having to stop.

Two officers flagged him down. Six noticed four others standing under a tree next to a white two-door Ford pickup labelled ZRP in big blue letters. It was close to 5:00 p.m. and most of them would be clocking off for the day. Six slowed down to a stop past the two orange drums in the road.

Two officers approached and asked him to open the trunk. He popped the latch. There wasn't much —only his backpack, and a 24-pack of natural spring water.

The officers tried to create a case out of thin air, harping on imaginary missing details on Six's international driving permit. They were curious why an international traveler didn't state fluency in any language. Officially, Six had only a backpack, a phone, and wallet with a U.S. $100 bill, which he knew he shouldn't have been carrying outside of a major city. The cops held on to his wallet and backpack, and found the U.S. passport that said his name was James George.

"Where were you coming from?" the cop said. "Harare?" The cop lifted a layer of dust from the car door with his finger. "And where are you going?"

"To see my grandmother. She is not feeling well."

"You're not from around here, are you? Where does your grandmother live?"

"In Chipinge."

The cop once again scrutinized the international driving permit, then handed it back to Six. He seemed disappointed.

The policeman searched Six's car and found a few filthy, tattered U.S. dollars, worn down like cloth.

"Where did you get these?"

"Change from the toll gate. Don't really know if I can use them anywhere else."

The officer chuckled. "That's what happens when your currency goes to shit, and you adopt a foreign currency as your own. You can't print the money, so use whatever is in the country until it's unusable. Do you have any more cash?"

Six sighed. "I do."

Six yanked open the passenger side door and showed the man a brick of five thousand American dollars he had withdrawn in Harare.

"That's a lot of cash," the other policeman said. "Where is the receipt?"

"I didn't take one, but I can show you the transaction from my bank on my phone," said Six, but his phone was dead.

"Why do you need this amount of cash?"

"Learned my lesson last time I was here. You guys know how it is in these little towns. Had to stand in line for four hours, only to be told the bank didn't have enough cash. Only wanted fifty U.S. dollars that time. This time I decided to get all the money I need for this trip at a bigger bank in the capital city."

The cop ordered Six to get out of the car with

his hands up. Six did not want to get out; several of the officers had surrounded the car now, two with assault rifles pointed at him. An officer who seemed higher in rank came out of the ZRP truck, and they handed him the brick.

"Out of the car now!"

"Okay. Okay." Six raised his hands. The cop opened the door, and Six got out and leaned on the car driver's side. Three men forced his hands behind his back and zip-tied his hands. They forced him onto the ground. They seemed to enjoy exercising power over him.

"I'm not fighting. Can someone tell me what's going on?"

The boss cop said, "Have these bills been washed?"

"How should I know?"

"Look at the color on your money." The man pointed to a spot with his finger.

Six looked at the bill more closely. He searched for the band's I.D. It was discolored with what looked like red nail polish. "I see it."

"It is dye residue. Most banks use this as a security measure. When someone robs their cash vault, the dye explodes and renders the money useless. The banks are insured, so they are covered for such losses."

"What does that have to do with me?"

"The money you have is from a bank that was robbed last week!"

"Why would I be traveling with a pile of robbed cash?"

"You tell us! No one travels with this amount of cash here."

"I need it to pay for my grandmother's hospital bill."

"Hospital bill, you say? Where?"

"In Chipinge."

"We shall see about that."

"Gents, I think there is a misunderstanding," Six said.

"You tell that to the judge!"

Six was forced into the bed of the small pickup truck by the four police officers who had been standing beneath the tree. This was the only time he had broken his $100 bill travel rule, and of course this was the only time he got stopped, searched, and arrested.

They arrived at the police station before the sun went down. The ride was rough in the dusty road, particularly for Six, with his hands behind his back. The cops looked at him as if he were a criminal. Six was offloaded at the station's front entrance and led to the front desk. Several other people with hands cuffed behind their backs were seated in the room, waiting.

The female officer at the desk recorded Six's belongings and stuffed everything into a paper bag: A wooden club. Two tee-shirts, two pairs of khaki shorts and one pair of chinos, underwear, three pairs of socks, sneakers, a pair of army boots and the $100 bill from his wallet. Where the $5000 brick had gone he did not know.

The officer never said a word, but the look of derision on her face said a thousand words. She loathed him. The cops had told him an organized crime syndicate had so far robbed six banks across the country and killed several people, including police officers, and was still running loose. Six understood why everyone was angry.

Then there was a commotion as another prisoner was brought in, cursing and resisting. The two cops dragging him in tried to force him into a chair. Then there was a gunshot.

"He shot himself! He shot himself!" Among the seated prisoners there was instant pandemonium and screaming.

"Get his gun!"

In the confusion Six had a chance to shed his own zip-tied handcuffs and rushed to help the flailing guy on the floor who was choking in his own blood, trying to speak. Six pressed the man's carotid artery. The man gargled some words. Six thought he understood and ought to remember. Blood gushed from the bullet hole below the man's jaw.

"The bullet severed his trachea," Six said to the officers surrounding him. "There is nothing anyone can do."

And it was true. By the time the ambulance arrived, the cleanup had been started and witness statements were being taken and the prisoner's body was cooling. Six was handcuffed with metal cuffs and written up for attempted escape.

"Can I make a call?" Six asked the desk officer.

She had a phone brought to Six at the corner of the room in the waiting area. Six spoke the phone number into the phone.

"Reggie, I have a number for you. Write it down."

"Where are you?"

"Listen, I only have a few minutes."

Six explained to Reggie.

"You got it?"

"I got it."

"Thanks, Reggie."

Six told the phone to end the call.

CHAPTER
FIVE

SIX WAS DETAINED, given a prison uniform in place of his bloody clothes, and the next day, handcuffed, was transferred to a jail in Chimanimani, a small growth point in the Eastern Highlands of Zimbabwe. The jail was next to a prison formerly used to hold Italian prisoners. He had heard a lot about this isolated prison in the mountains, built in the 1930s by the Rhodesian government to incarcerate notorious criminals. It was a gulag for Italian prisoners in the 1960s under the Rhodesian government. The Italians were used to build the narrow Chimanimani road carved into the mountainside. It wound around and through the treacherous mountain passes so often susceptible to avalanches and mud slides because of the torrential rainfalls in the region.

The holding facility was divided into two: One section for petty offenses and another for serious crimes. Most people behind bars in the first section were allowed out into the courtyard, to play some soccer, bask in the sun, or watch some local sports on the old black-and-white TV in their dining area.

The latter section was reserved for suspects accused of more serious crimes such as armed robberies, rape, and murder. Six was in that section. These prisoners were hardened, previous offenders who had found their way back to prison for their second or third run. Barely any amenities. The services you received were inversely proportional to your offense. Fights broke out daily. Loads of men in crammed spaces with loads of testosterone, in a confined space all day with no work to do. There was not even an old black-and-white TV. No books. Some prisoners were as young as sixteen. Stupid. The instinct was to always size each other up and assert dominance. That was human nature. It was difficult on weekends when these prisoners could hear the petty criminals from the other section outdoors playing soccer.

Six sat in his corner, trying to stay warm with a cover sheet. Winter was approaching and this thin cloth proved useless as a blanket. Today was Sunday. It had been a week since Six had been brought to this place. His arraignment had been scheduled at the local magistrate court, but had been postponed twice, and the next time was two days away. He sat all day, doing nothing. Two meals a day—porridge in the morning, then *sadza* with cabbage, beans, soy chunks, or *matemba*, tiny dried fish from the Kariba dam, in the evening. That was it. *Sadza* was a local staple made from boiled maize-meal, stirred until thick to hold in one's hand. Six worried that the longer he stayed here, the more malnourished he would become, and the more insane he would get. No wonder fights broke out daily.

Six had been in challenging situations both in

the marines and as a contractor, but the peculiar thing about this place was, being here you knew there was no hope, only despair. This was a place you could disappear into, and no one would ever know you existed. Most people in here seemed resigned to their fate, although he witnessed one or two emotional breakdowns over the week. Usually, the seemingly physically stronger ones broke down first. The system didn't care about people here since they were not convicts yet, so the budget was low. He had heard the situation didn't get any better for those convicted. The government didn't care. Convicts were considered a waste to societal resources. A few inmates with relatives close by received good food from the outside.

After three postponements Six was placed in remand with one meal per day, dirty services, and a three-gallon bucket in the corner, the contents of which he dumped every morning into the common toilet when his cell door was opened. They wouldn't let him empty it any more than that. Most of the prisoners preferred being in the penitentiary to being in remand.

To keep his sanity, he spent the days stretching, doing pull-ups, push-ups, and isometric holds using the wall and metal bars. Mastering every inch of his body. It kept him from going crazy. No equipment needed.

THE NOON BELL RANG. The inmates lined up in the communal eating area for their single meal of the day. The first plate of cold *sadza* and boiled vegetables slid through the lower gap below the metal doors. Everyone hesitated.

Six was so famished he made the mistake of stepping out of line and picked up the plate, and then several other men scrambled to get theirs, and the guards hollered for order. The meal had tasted the same for the last seven days. Cold *sadza* with stale kale, salty and boiled to wet shreds, on one lucky day cooked with some tomatoes and another lucky day with the tiny salted *matemba* fish. Which had been only once. The whole prison had a filthy human stench after days and weeks of no bathing. Nobody cared. The guards enjoyed tormenting their captives. It seemed that most people here had signed off their right to be treated as humans.

As Six was eating, four men approached his table. Two older, and two young. The one in the lead towered over the others, taller than Six; Six guessed the guy was about six feet seven inches tall. It mattered: Height made the guy an easier target. The second one was about the same height as Six. The last two were shorter. They approached him in that pecking order. The big man said to Six, "Light skin bitch!"

Six ignored him.

"Do you hear me, bitch?"

Six looked up from his plate. "Where did you learn that? Gangster movies?"

"What are you gonna do about it?"

"Go do games to someone else." Six took a bite of his *sadza*, dismissing their presence.

"Or what? Are you threatening me?"

Six sat up straight quickly, was aware that the wall was behind him. His sudden movement made the shorter two men flinch backwards.

"Look, I'm already angry and you are just pissing me off more. I'm going to give you two choices."

"What choices?"

"One, you eat your food in that corner, and two, you behave like little boys somewhere else out of my face."

"We gonna teach you a lesson!"

"Aren't you guys supposed to be doing something useful with your life?"

"Keep talking!"

"Okay," Six said, placing the empty metal plate just ahead of him. "Either way, I'll crush you. Now get out of my face."

The men scoffed. Then they looked at each other, weighing the odds.

"Who put you up to this?" said Six. "You tell me who sent you, and I'll let you walk out of here in one piece."

Six guessed the two younger men were barely out of high school, with soft stubble showing on their faces.

"How old are you?" Six said to them. "You look like your mom just finished breastfeeding you last year."

The young man's eyebrows scrunched together, and his lips tightened. "You think you're funny, huh?"

Six laughed. "For real though, look at this guy—"

The man swung at Six before he finished the sentence. Six was ready. He blocked the man's arm with the metal plate, then used it to slam the arm onto the wooden table. The man winced in pain, holding his hand. "Fuck, you just broke my hand!"

"I never touched you."

His comrades surrounded and tried to jump him. Six pushed the table towards them in one move, knocking the shortest two to the floor. One got up in a daze and attacked, wrapping his hands around Six and slamming him into the wall. Six hammered the man's back with his elbow. The man loosened his grip and Six sucker-punched him in the face, breaking his nose, and a tooth flew out. It hurt Six's hand.

The big man swung his right arm at Six's head. Six blocked the man's punch with his left, at the same time planting his fist into the man's abdomen, and then a left to the jaw. He followed this with a hard right-leg kick to the chest, sending him plummeting into his comrades to the floor. The big man hit the concrete with a thud. He stayed there motionless. The last man standing flew at Six. Six met the man's face with a flying hook kick. The man flipped backwards, his head hitting the edge of the wooden table. Then he tumbled to the ground and did not move.

Six could feel his breath quicken. "You pissed me off!"

The commotion in the dining hall had made the guards on duty call for backup. Several guards surrounded Six, then handcuffed him, and only then handcuffed each of the four bloody men.

One of the guards, whose badge said Officer Jade, dragged Six into the hallway. She told Six, "I saw what happened. Do not make any more trouble. I think it's safe now for the other detainees. Make sure nothing like this happens again while you are here."

"They need to leave me alone!"

"I know, but we must take you to a separate cell now. Maybe for your own good. You have enemies now. Most guys in here have cliques. You mess with any one of them, you'd better be ready for all of them."

"Who put them up to this?"

She moved closer to Six. "You have some powerful enemies, Mr. George." She paused and looked into Six's face. "I know you didn't rob any banks. You are not even from around here. "

"What enemies?"

"I might lose my job for saying this. It's the mayor. We overheard a call last night. From Mayor Hove. If I recall, you put Hove in jail not many months ago."

Six looked at her, feigning surprise.

Officer Jade continued, "Every cop here knows you now. What you did to the Mayor and his cronies in Vic Falls."

Six paused. "I remember. What did he want?"

"He wanted you dead. But none of us officers want to kill anyone inside, so some bribe inmates to do the job for some extra favors."

"Why are you telling me this?"

"Some of us joined the force to do good. I know some are corrupt, but most are still good. We still stand for what's right. I read what you and Detective Kona did in Vic Falls. I know you can do something about it."

This time her hand was hooked to his. Six nodded.

"So, the guys were bribed by the mayor?"

"Yes."

"Isn't he in prison right now?"

"He is in prison all right," she said. "A comfy

twin bed of his choice and tailored meals, a flat-screen TV with movie and cable subscription. Guards on his payroll. And he's still the mayor. I'd say he is doing very well."

"The system is corrupt."

Six was led into a separate section of the facility more secluded from the rest. At least it was away from the wailing of other inmates having break-downs. This place was quiet. Officer Jade opened the door to his new cell.

"I think the judge has confirmed your trial will go on tomorrow," the officer said.

"I'll believe that when it happens."

She locked the metal door behind herself and left.

KARIM ARRIVED EARLY for the meeting at the Mendoubia Gardens, a seven-minute walk from his hotel in downtown Tangier. He was curious what the response would be after the failed mission in Tangier. But he wasn't scared. He was never scared. He was meeting his controller here for mission update. Karim knew his missions could be daily, weekly, or once a year. Anywhere. It didn't matter. He had to be available whenever duty called.

He chose a spot on the grass where he could see anyone coming up the hill. Mostly families strolling, children playing soccer, and taxis parked along the street below. He browsed through the morning newspaper, mainly looking at pictures and captions. There were no reports about the Royal Tulip hotel murder. He felt slightly disappointed to not find a story about the death.

The woman arrived about ten minutes later, a woman in dark glasses, blue jeans, and a green hoodie and a backpack. Karim watched over the newspaper as she approached him. She removed her earphones and sat down across from him.

She said, "The boss is mad. You failed."

"Info was wrong," Karim said.

"It's your job to verify your sources."

He nodded.

She retrieved an envelope from her backpack and slid it across the table to him.

"Here are your new orders. Your new target."

"Tell me about the target."

"It's in Addis Ababa three days from now. All the details and plan are in the envelope. Support team will be provided."

Karim broke the seal and opened the envelope. He checked the papers and images, and the map for the attack.

"Madame, that's a lot of people. I've always pushed bribes and kickbacks, but this is going to hurt innocent people—children."

"Do you always question your orders?"

"No, Madame."

"Then do your job. I wonder what your father will say if I mention your questioning."

Karim continued perusing the papers.

The woman said, "These are desperate times, my dear. Sometimes they require desperate measures."

He looked away.

"Do whatever is necessary. Unless you want to be eliminated. I can find another person to replace you."

"Understood." Karim pointed at the photo of his target." Who is this one? What is this document I'm supposed to get?"

"None of your business. You do your job."

Karim remained quiet. He had his suspicions. Whoever was ordering these targets had to be high up. Maybe the French foreign affairs minister, or someone high-ranking in the intelligence agency. He couldn't imagine exactly who. He didn't care. He wondered what his next victim's crime was. Possibly none. But his employers would kill just because they could. Again, his job was to follow instructions and kill. He flipped to the next page where details about his target were outlined.

"Don't fail your father again, Karim!"

She put on her shades and walked away.

CHAPTER
SEVEN

Two weeks earlier

SIX, a former U.S. Marine, was unofficially employed by NEPHRON, a private covert contract organization that handled issues like corruption and human trafficking as well as hunting down international criminals across the globe. Six's target area was Africa. The organization included field operatives, accountants, programmers, hackers, drivers, and safe houses. NEPHRON was capable of hacking some of the most secure computer systems in the world. They could sieve through some of the complex shell companies and crime syndicates. In past missions they had successfully hunted down war criminals and infiltrated underground financial corporations. They had brought down dictators in Sri Lanka, Venezuela, Nigeria, Angola, and more recently Six had helped put corrupt Zimbabwean leaders behind bars.

On his off days, Six liked to stay off the grid to clear his mind, if that were ever possible. Traveling did expand his horizons, taught him not to stress too much. In all these places, no one knew who he was and no one cared. He liked that. As an American expat, traveling in Europe was easy. He liked to go to Europe, the Riviera, and just explore beauty, often alternating between the Italian side and the French side. It was therapy for him. Beautiful. It was a habit from his early days when he was stationed in Germany in the Marines. He would often take the train for a weekend when he left the base. *The good old days,* Six thought, remembering the escapades he and his buddies had in those parts of the continent. He smiled at the fond memories.

He had spent a few days in the French Riviera then took a train north to Lyon. Six finished his morning full-body workout at the hotel fitness center, then took a cold shower. He had found the ice-cold shower helped him recover more quickly.

The spring weather was perfect for May, with a warm early-morning breeze welcoming summer. The weather was neither too hot nor cold, the breeze just right. Six decided to walk along the narrow, paved street to a local café he had found in the hotel brochure, just down the street. The café was famous for its creativity, mixing the old with the new. It was well known for its tradition and simplicity. The boulangerie still made bread as it was made when the café was founded back in the days of King Louis XVI and Napoleon Bonaparte. Six thought that sounded pretty good. Fewer preservatives and processing. "Enriched flour" and all— none of that crap. He marveled at the buildings leeward across the river Rhône. The streets were still empty at this time. Not for long. Soon the streets would be clogged by thousands of tourists flocking into the area from Mediterranean cruise ships that docked in the afternoons.

A few blocks later, he arrived at the café, a spot frequented by white-collar Parisians for breakfast and lunch. Picturesque. The interior was the image of a 1920s French restaurant. One of the few buildings that still valued style, Six thought.

The place was busy but not too crowded. Six waited at the counter.

"Will be right with you in a minute, Sir," the barista said, while finishing pushing down on the espresso lever. Moments later, she placed two cold-brewed teas on the pickup counter and called out, "Two mango chais!"

Six watched as a couple picked up the order and retreated to the rustic lounge chairs.

Six ordered a regular latte with no sugar, and an original baguette. The mochas and any item with chocolate tended to give him gas, and he avoided them at all costs. He watched as the barista prepared the latte. Six picked it up in less than three minutes. He retreated to a chair in the café courtyard garden. The coffee tasted great.

Moments later, a woman walked in. From the way she walked and interacted with the barista, Six guessed she must have been a regular.

"What culinary delights do you have for me today?" the woman said.

"Soup."

"Oh, soup. What kind?"

"Tomato basil."

"Nice. But what else would you recommend?"

"An almond croissant."

"I'll take that. With a white-chocolate mocha."

"Right on."

The woman tipped the barista and sat two tables away from Six in the courtyard, but facing him, and laid down a book and a magazine.

He gazed at the woman in front of him. He preferred to keep to himself. He enjoyed being alone, but he found himself drawn to her. He tried to stave off the thought. He also knew sexual discipline made him who he was, in a world perverted by lust and instant gratification. A few of the women he met were a waste of his time and not worth the free validation from him. He couldn't. He glanced towards her again after a waiter brought her croissant and coffee. There was a peculiar energy about her in the way she sat upright, the way she bit into the almond croissant and gracefully sipped. She glanced his direction just at the same time and their eyes locked for a few prolonged seconds. She smiled and brushed a strand of hair behind her ear. Six liked it. He smiled back.

Unbeknownst to Six, the woman had been watching him as well. She wore a grey beret. Old school, but she liked it. There was something cool about wearing one, and an autumn sleeveless dress. That was her vibe. She set down the remaining half of the almond croissant and felt the ceramic cup with her mocha in both of her hands. This was a very special drink. Her favorite. And the blooming flowers in the garden. She had chosen a seat in the café garden that let her see the inside of the café. There were only a few patrons in the garden at this time, but she knew that within an hour or so, the place would be packed. Only locals frequented this place earlier in the day, or foreigners who cared enough to find out. She thought it was the best. She crossed her legs, revealing just enough of her thighs. She sipped on her coffee seemingly distracted by her phone, then laid it down and opened the magazine on the table. She could see him, though. After all these years she was a pro at this. She knew tactics that would turn even the red-pilled and self-proclaimed "alphas" into simps. She understood what men like him wanted. Her intelligence report had said so. He had the looks to get whatever he wanted; women were constantly falling into his lap. Entitled women, or trashy, shallow, classy, and every type of woman you could name. But she knew he had always been a principled guy. Everyone in his circle knew of his integrity. While many women fell head over heels for him, he had remained strong. No one knew which women he was dating or courting. He was generous, handsome, charismatic, and ripped. The complete package. Yet no woman had managed to lock him down, even though he was twenty-eight. She sipped her coffee while observing. She knew what he wanted: a little sophistication and culture. In a world where everything was superficial, guys like himself had a sixth sense for the red flags of superficial women. Frankly, he had much to lose by choosing the wrong partner. An empire was resting on his shoulders right now.

She watched him make a beeline to her table. She kept her gaze planted in the magazine.

"What are you reading?"

The woman looked up and smiled.

"Stephen King has a short story in here." He noticed her drawled French accent.

She showed the magazine cover to Six and said, "Do you know *Shawshank Redemption*?"

"I've watched the movie."

"That's one of his stories."

"I'm Six, by the way."

"I'm Ophélie. Six, as in Six—?"

"Draye Sixpence."

"Nice to meet you Six," she said, extending a hand, which he shook firmly.

"Nice to meet you too, Ophélie."

The barista called his name, and he went to pick up his baguette and returned to her table.

"This is the best coffee I've had in a while," he said, smiling.

She smiled back and said, "It's the best coffee shop in town."

"May I?" Six pointed at the empty chair next to her.

"Sure," she said. Then she went back to reading.

"*Meditations* by Marcus Aurelius, huh?" he said, observing the book lying on the table.

"You've read it?"

"Yes. I like all works by the Stoics."

"Me too. I find it useful in today's world where everyone is a victim. And we are bombarded by propaganda from every angle."

He nodded. "Fair enough."

"Where are you from?"

"I travel around," he said, folding his left leg. "I hear an accent. *Vous êtes Française?*"

"*Oui!* Is that obvious?" She swiped her long hair away from her face.

"I have heard quite a few French accents, I guess."

She simpered and straightened her hair. "*Et toi?*"

"No. Just a guy who likes languages," he said, noticing her provocative light-brown eyes.

"Nice. Reading helps improve my English." She pointed at the book.

"Your English is great."

"Thank you."

"Which part of France?"

"Yvoire."

Six nodded, although he didn't know where this was.

"It's a village right next to Switzerland. I spent most of my childhood in the south of France, though."

"How's it there?"

"It's beautiful. I miss it there."

"I just came from the Riviera."

Her eyes shone. "You've been there?"

"Yes. I love it there."

She loosened a bit, uncrossed her long legs, and switched them to right over left, and rested the magazine on the table. "That's so cool."

"You grew up there?"

"Yes. Born in Eritrea. Parents moved to France when I was four."

"Cool."

Six was struck by her lush body. He watched her caramel skin that merged well with her thick, lush dark curls. Crystal brown eyes. With a coyness that commanded desire and respect at the same time. She finished the croissant with grace, savoring each bite.

"The name Ophélie. Your parents must have been big Shakespeare fans."

"They were. I see you're well read."

"A little bit. I like a lot of things. For Shakespeare I didn't have a choice. They made me read it in school. I hated it."

They laughed.

A waiter who had been watching them came by and asked if Ophélie would like a glass of water. She told him she was fine and wanted nothing more today.

"First time in Lyon?" Six said.

"No. My parents used to bring me here every summer."

"That's awesome. Any place you would recommend visiting around here?"

"Any place in particular?"

"Humor me."

"Give me a ballpark of what interests you."

"Anything food and art."

"You've come to the right place. We have it all: cathedrals, museums, Roman amphitheaters, and the best food."

"I didn't know that."

"I like to call it the food capital of France."

"What a coincidence."

"I was going to do some grocery shopping at the food market." She checked her watch. "Right now. The Uber is coming."

"Care if I tag along?"

"Sure. Why not? It's fun with more people. I could show you a couple places. I have some time."

"Lucky me. I get to have my own personal guide."

"Two hundred Euros per hour."

"I don't know if I can afford that. Any discount?"

"For you, sir, two percent."

"Do you accept credit?"

"Nope, cash only."

Six frowned.

"But since this is your first time, my good sir, I will give you the tour for free."

"Merci."

They laughed.

"Okay, then, let's go. The Uber is almost here."

They walked out and boarded a black Mazda.

AFTER A FEW HOURS EXPLORING, Six and Ophélie grabbed lunch at noon at a local cozy family-owned *bouchon* along the streets in the older part of town overlooking the river Saône. They sat side by side at the bar, liking the view toward the river.

After lunch they walked along the riverwalk toward the taxi. Six helped Ophélie with her grocery bags.

Six said, "How come a woman like you is not in a relationship?"

She looked taken aback by the question.

"I'm a straightforward guy. It saves both of us time not to play games."

She laughed. "I like that, actually."

"So?"

"It's complicated. I just got out of a long-term relationship."

"Taking time to heal?"

"Yes. What better way than to explore corners of France?"

"I'd feel as if being here makes it hurt more."

"Not for me. It makes me realize there is more

to life. I could read, drink good coffee, run in the streets, eat good food—and just be alive."

"I can see that," Six said.

"What about you?" she said.

"I move around a lot," Six said. He pointed to his backpack.

"Let me guess. Everything you own is in that pack."

"Yes. The lighter, the better."

"I like that. Are you in a relationship?"

"No."

"Why do I doubt that? A guy like you couldn't be single."

"I could, but I choose not to."

Ophélie leaned in to kiss him. Six stopped her.

"Look, you are a very beautiful woman. You've been through a lot recently, and I don't want to add to that trauma. Take your time, heal, I know you'll find your guy soon enough."

"I'm sorry. I just thought—"

"Don't be. I like this too. But then what? I will just add more hurt to what you already feel. I'm just not ready for flings."

He drew her closer, looked her in the eyes. She leaned on his chest. He hugged her.

"I enjoyed our time together," Six said. "Maybe it will work out in the future."

She nodded slowly.

"I'll hit you up next time I'm in France."

They hugged. Six kissed her on the forehead.

"Take care of yourself, Six."

"You, too." Six flagged her a taxi, opened the door for her, and watched the car disappear into the streets.

Six got back to his hotel room late. There was a

voicemail from Grandma Grace informing him that she was in a hospital and that his distant cousin was in jail for theft. Grandma Grace was Six's paternal grandmother, one of the few close relatives he had left or knew. She lived in a small village in Zimbabwe.

CHAPTER
EIGHT

SIX SAT up on the sheet, leaning on the cold concrete wall. He yawned and stretched. The ray of light through the slit in the wall signaled it was Monday morning. His back felt like a rod from sleeping on the concrete, with the paper-thin cloth for a blanket. Despite the soreness, he had slept well. His days in the Marines had conditioned him to sleep anywhere—on rock, dirt, concrete, or flooded areas. The separate room, a solitary-confinement cell, was all concrete, which was cold during early winter in May.

A worn-out, dented metal bowl of cornmeal porridge was slid under the door. Six guessed it must be around 10:00 or 11:00 a.m. He observed the bowl's contents deliberating whether to eat them. He was hungry. It was loose, lukewarm, tasteless, with no sugar. Six drank the porridge. It went down easier that way.

He waited. Any moment now the door would open, and he would be handcuffed, dragged, and loaded into the open bed of an old UD truck to the courthouse with many others in remand. Rain or shine. Same routine.

At first Six had thought he would be in remand for a day or two. But now, even after a week, he saw no hope. So far, the arraignment had been postponed three times. He had learned from the guards that two of those times, the judge was on vacation, and the last one, the judge had been called up last minute to the capital. The sequence was the same. The prisoners were loaded into trucks, driven miles to court in shackles, only to be notified the local magistrate was sick or was on vacation. The judges here owned the law and did whatever they wanted. Often taking bribes on the side. And those white wigs they wore. Bastards.

He hoped the fourth time would be a charm. He had chosen to represent himself in court. He didn't know how they would react when he pleaded not guilty of possessing the stolen bills, because he had his suspicions about justice here. He hoped he would get the information he needed soon.

The heavy metal outer door creaked open, and Six heard footsteps approaching his cell. Officer Jade opened the door and motioned Six out. Six walked into the hallway for the first time without being handcuffed.

"What's going on?"

"You're free to go."

"But I haven't had a trial yet."

"The boss said you are out."

The officer led Six to the lobby, passing through several holding cell areas. They talked.

"Your charges have been dropped," Officer Jade said. "You have been acquitted of all potential charges. I don't know how you did it, but that phone call you made really stirred things up and caused waves."

"What am I missing?"

"There has been a police shakedown. Including the local district magistrate. Someone is here to see you."

"Who? I don't know anyone around here."

"I don't know who it is."

Officer Jade told him that the bank robbers had been caught and killed attempting another robbery in a different city.

"Is that why I'm being released?"

"Partly, but word came from above. You have friends in high places."

Officer Jade looked around, then at Six, then down. She didn't say a word.

"Of course," Six said. "Looks as if the department is saving its tail. That's why they wanted me dead!"

"There has been a station shakedown. Several police officers and the magistrate were part of the robbery scheme," Officer Jade said. "Whoever you called said the right words."

"I should find out why Mayor Hove had me jailed."

"Just leave it. You can't clean everything."

"I know. But how can a country prosper when even the people sworn to protect the law abuse it?"

"Corruption is everywhere here, from the store cashier, teachers, officers, to the President. The other day I was ordering some documents printed and the cashier wanted an extra two dollars on the side to get them printed quickly and notarized. It's crazy!"

"How can you solve that amount of corruption?"

"Sometimes it requires people like you."

Six looked at her.

Officer Jade continued, "And sometimes force is the answer. These corrupt bastards are like nose hair. You cut them and they keep coming back. Annoying. Always the only way the country will turn around is when a new president is ruthless from the top down. Everyone needs to pay for their shit. Ministers, governors, M.P.s, D.A.s, land officers, everyone."

Six saw that the demeanor of several of the guards had changed. Officer Jade handed Six his belongings via the thick plastic barricade. Six collected his five thousand American dollars at the front lobby and signed out from the tattered logbook on the counter. He was handed his backpack. Six checked the contents. All items were there and intact: his few belongings and his club and cellphone.

The guard escorted him out of the exit into the searing midday sun.

REGGIE WAS STANDING beside her jeep, hands in her jeans' front pockets, wearing sunglasses.

"To whom do I owe this surprise?" Six said, squinting in the bright sunlight.

Reggie smiled. "Not me. I would've preferred you rot in jail."

"And that would make your life complete?"

"Yes. Just personal satisfaction."

Even under the shades, Six could see Reggie's cheerful big brown eyes. Reggie, a former detective for the Central Investigation Department (CID), was now employed by the African Union Intelligence and Law Enforcement Bureau (AULEB). Teaming up with Six, she and he had solved the high-profile case of missing children just a few months prior. AULEB was responsible for maintaining peace across the continent, regardless of borders and nationalities. It could operate anywhere in the continent. Reggie was a field agent.

She said, "Had to help a Prince Charming in distress."

"It's usually the other way around."

Reggie gave him a peck on the cheek and frowned. "You smell like shit."

"They don't have showers in there."

"You need to shower ASAP!" Reggie said, furrowing her nose.

"Can we leave this hellhole now?"

She patted his shoulder. "Hop in. We have a long drive. Just being here gives me the creeps."

Six gave one last look at the place that had been his home for the last twelve days. He gazed at the guard towers over the coiled barbed wire wrapped above the fifteen-foot brick wall that fortressed the jail.

When seated, Six said, "Thank you. And thanks for the money. Was sure I'd never see it again."

"You're welcome."

They barreled down the narrow gravel strip, leaving clouds of dust.

Six lowered both windows to let fresh air in. Reggie flared her nostrils. "That's better. I was going to pass out."

"Nice manly stench."

Reggie kept her eyes on the road, navigating a few potholes.

"So how did you find me?" Six said.

"It wasn't hard after you phoned. Follow the trail of police records, and the station's area code."

"My back feels like a dead log," Six said to Reggie. "I fought four guys yesterday." Six told her all about the fight.

Reggie said, "How did the guys know you?"

"Someone on the outside wanted me dead, but they wanted their own hands clean. The guard said it might be Mayor Hove."

"The mayor from Vic Falls? I can see that guy carrying a vendetta."

"Still don't know how he knew I was here."

"Everything is now being digitized into a national database. But their cyber-security is still decades backwards, so it's easy for anyone to hack the system. Someone hacked in, found you, and called them to eliminate you. Thankfully police here still don't carry guns around."

They drove in silence for a while.

Six retrieved his watch, put it on and buckled the wristband.

"What time is it?" Six said.

"Quarter past three," Reggie said, reading from her fitness tracker.

"Thanks. Mine is off. Two fifty-five. I have to set the time every now and then."

Six turned the watch stem to 3:16.

"I have always seen you with that watch. You never take it off."

"It's a vintage piece, and I like collectibles." Six

used his shirt to wipe the watch's worn-out glass and silver casing.

Reggie smiled. "You should get a new one."

"It was my dad's. He gifted it to me when I was seven. Only thing I've left from him. Originally belonged to my grandfather. It's my lucky charm." Six chuckled.

"Never took you for the sentimental type."

"It has been through hell with me—fights, crashes, underwater, now jail, and here it stands. It's also different. No one uses these anymore. It works anywhere. No electronics. Doesn't need batteries or charging. You just set the dial and crank the stem. Can last for eons compared to any of the modern stuff."

"Now," said Reggie, "you owe me one." Reggie explained to Six that the prisoner who killed himself in the police station was part of a team that had robbed several gas stations and two banks, killing four people. Reggie had uncovered the ring of police officers involved with them and also in the Triple Z drug trade, and more recent local bank robberies. Several police chiefs who were part of the crime ring were all behind bars now, and a dozen robbers, but the clearly organized robberies spanning all of Africa had continued. Corrupt police officers had to be involved.

"I hate bullies," she said. "But I have to thank you. The numbers you got from the dead guy were a passcode for a Barclays safe deposit box in Mutare. Once we figured that out, it was easy to get a warrant and our agents in Mutare to check the place. Turns out that guy had dossiers on all the corrupt cops and politicians he did dirty business with. He probably knew his days were numbered."

"They left him with a gun to shoot himself?"

"To appear as an accident. No one questions or cares if a criminal shoots himself.

"There is more. Some of them were willing to sell other members in exchange for shorter prison sentences. We found out that the new Reserve Bank Governor was involved in illegal forex trading, mainly in U.S. dollars. Those guys you see outside grocery stores offering to swipe a credit card for you using the local currency in exchange for U.S. dollar cash. He had a deal with some banks to supply those credit cards."

"Didn't we just nail the old governor just a few months ago?"

"We did."

"So how's that even possible?"

"He runs the reserve bank. He manufactures more credit cards. And as you know credit cards are not actually money. So he was making money out of thin air."

"What happens to him?"

"He was arrested at his home yesterday."

"You think he will go to prison?"

Reggie laughed. "He won't. That's how corrupt things are here. He won't even make it into the papers in Harare. But he will lose his job."

Six rubbed his fists together and looked out the window.

Reggie spoke. "But our guys at the Bureau are doing whatever we can to make sure he eventually ends up behind bars."

"You think he will?"

"He will. Our powers are different than local law authorities. We can't be threatened or bought."

Reggie and Six had been partners solving activities in Vic Falls, and Reggie as the lead detective had been promoted to chief of the Bureau's Southern Africa office in Johannesburg. But she had chosen to stay in the field instead. She had confided this information to Six but would not tell Six exactly what she did now. "If I did I'd have to kill you," she explained.

"I see the new gig comes with better wheels. Not bad." Six eyed the Land Cruiser.

"I can put in a word for you, you know. The team will like you."

"Thanks, but no thanks. I like where I am now."

"Tell me, why the heck are you here? It's like chaos follows you."

"My grandmother is sick. My family is here."

"Did you see her?"

"Not yet. Those guys found me as I was on my way. The rental company took my car at the police station. Someone wanted me dead."

"The Bureau needs you before this whole thing blows out of proportion."

"Why me? Why not the FBI or MI6?" Six said.

"We must solve our own crimes for once on our own. No spoon-feeding. And whatever those organizations do, there are strings attached."

"They have the resources, though," Six said.

"Agreed. But we also do. I know with your help we can find the perpetrators."

"Busy with solving several recent mass attacks across the continent."

"The higher-ups want you to help with the attacks that have been happening."

"I'm not doing shit for you guys!" Six said. "Look where doing good got me."

"Please? Will you? You owe me one."

"Fine. I'll help."

She reached into her jeans pocket and handed Six a badge. "You are my assistant."

Six smiled. "Just like old times, huh?"

"You are all set."

"You really planned this. Do I have a choice?"

"Nope. You don't have a way out of this one."

"Where do we start?"

CHAPTER
NINE

SIX AND REGGIE drove for a while in silence while Six fiddled with the car stereo. None of the local channels worked. The mountains in these parts of the country tended to distort both telecommunication and radio signals. Six gave up.

"About what happened last time in Vic Falls," Six said.

"What?"

"Sorry, we got carried away the last time we were together."

"I know, but nothing happened."

"Yes and no."

"It was just a kiss."

"A passionate kiss," Six said. "Look, I like you a lot, but I also value you as a person. More than sex. I like who you are."

"What does that mean?"

"If I'm going to make this work, I must do it right. That's just what I believe, and I don't bend those rules. Not for anyone. I don't want to be carrying around regrets and memories I wish I could forget."

"What does 'do it right' mean?"

"I have to marry you first."

Reggie looked at him. "I knew you were raised right! Is that Grandma Grace's doing?"

"You could say that. Let's say I like my character to be consistent. What I do in private is same as what I do in public."

"I like that! Sorry if I came off as loose. I have never done that before."

"I know," Six said.

An hour later, they turned right onto the highway. A few kilometers down the road was a flea market. They parked outside the fence and walked inside. The place clamored with merchants selling used clothes, shoes, flip-flops, knock-off cellphones, gadgets—the clothes all fast fashion from the West and China, for men, women, children, and toddlers. Bales and bales of used clothes were delivered weekly from Beira port in Mozambique, and were piled ready for auctioning.

With no jobs in the country, locals came here and bid for cheap bales, which they would take inland to sell to support their families. Since the collapse of the country's textile industry, the country had become a dumping ground for used clothes—fast-fashion brands and even high-end American and European brands. The used clothing and electronics business was the only source of income for most of the population, and lucrative for a few. This market was a hub for thriving used-clothes businesses. All of it was garbage from the West. One man's garbage, another's treasure. The true meaning of that came alive in this place.

Bales, packed with clothes meant for landfills, but here they became gold. This influx crippled the local once-thriving textile industry. Who would want to buy a local handmade cotton shirt if they could get a branded used shirt at a fraction of the cost? The secondhand clothes industry was thriving so much that it had rendered the local textile industry obsolete.

Six and Reggie approached the first stall adjacent to the entrance. Clothes were piled on wooden platforms, some on do-it-yourself mannequins made of wood and plastic. The clothes were arranged in three piles: a pile for new or newish clothes, a pile for gently-used clothes, and a pile for scraps, such as underwear with holes. A pole with a cardboard displaying the prices stood next to each pile: five dollars, three dollars, and one dollar respectively. Reggie dug into the "newish" pile and picked a plain blue t-shirt. They dug in some more and found a pair of blue Levi jeans.

"I think these will fit," Reggie said, holding the t-shirt to Six.

He smelled it and coughed.

"I thought I smelled bad, but this—"

Reggie laughed. "Don't worry, the moisture should go away once the shirt gets some fresh air."

"Smells like a basement."

Six offered three dollars for the clothes which the vendor refused at first, but eventually relented when Six decided to move on to the next vendor.

Six gave the man a five-dollar bill. The man handed him two one-dollar bills. Six felt the tattered, soft, dirty bills in his hand.

When away from the stall, Six said, "How did I do?"

Reggie smiled. "Not bad. The price is never set

here. Can always haggle for a discount. Better to sell for cheap than keep unsold merchandise."

"I hope these are not moldy."

"After months in a container, some fresh air should do the trick."

Reggie bought several packs of chewing gum from a girl in a concession stall on the way out.

They snailed along the gravel road back into the highway, navigating roads dilapidated from erosion and damage.

"These roads are so bad," Reggie said.

"When your government hires foreign companies to build your roads instead of empowering local companies, they cut corners."

"But still."

"There is no regulation. The government leaders are responsible for making sure the companies build quality infrastructure, not thin sheets. They turn a blind eye and get kickbacks."

"All on borrowed money!"

"This shit never made sense to me," Reggie said. "We are always borrowing money from other countries. How do these other countries like China or the U.S. have the money?"

"They just print more money."

"Why can't we print our own money?"

"Inflation. Some countries have tried. Look at Zimbabwe. The system seems to be rigged against poor countries. I think both the IMF and World Bank benefit from this in the name of benevolence. Plus, our leaders want the easy way out disregarding the burden they are leaving for future generations."

"It pisses me off!"

"True. Most of it is due to corruption and mis-management. Greed."

"To change the country, you have to sack everyone in every branch of government," Reggie said. "It's rotten from top to bottom."

"That's exactly what one of the guards at the jail said."

"It's true. We have a system that disincentivizes education and hard work. All you need is political connections. That's why you see kids who are supposed to be in school out here selling stuff."

"Economic and social policies are designed to serve the political elite."

"It is a contentious topic," Reggie said.

"You've got elected leaders bilking the continent's resources for themselves, and multinational corporations exploiting locals. When has anything run by the government been good or efficient?" Six said.

"Fair point, but here politicians know they are untouchable. Good journalism is non-existent here."

"The state owns the media. The ruling party does. Anyone who speaks against the regime disappears," Reggie said.

"I see how much we take for granted back in the U.S.," said Six. "But at some point, the masses will revolt against the exploitation. It has always happened in history."

"They will. That's what happens when you screw up the social contract. At this point the masses have had enough. This is the perfect time. Most of the war veterans here who fought against the colonialists are dead or too old for politics. This leaves room for the young people to bring change.

The old bloods were driven by vengeance. But we want development, not reparations. My mom was a war veteran," Reggie said.

"Really?"

"She joined the guerrilla war in Mozambique when she was twelve."

"That's crazy. Too young."

"From her words, 'It was hypnotic. Kids left school to join and most never made it back. All for freedom.'"

"I hope that day comes soon."

They reached Mutare at sundown. Mutare was Zimbabwe's fourth largest city.

"Let's get some shuteye and tomorrow see your grandmother while we plan our next moves."

"You got a few days?"

"No," Reggie said. "But being out here, away from the city, might clear my mind and help me piece this puzzle together. I'm hoping to get up-dates from my superiors on what's next on the mission for me. And for you."

SEVERAL CITIES TO THE SOUTH, three men hauled cleaning equipment past the metal barricade that blocked the mall entrance from vehicle traffic. The men, in the familiar blue overalls worn by service workers at the Mall of Africa, got out of the utility van and entered the mall a floor below the main cafeteria. The electrical system needed to be assessed, perhaps repaired. They took the service elevator to the basement. The overalled men turned left and passed two patrol guards. They exchanged greetings. Due to load shedding, which happened randomly and frequently across the country, it was common to have people enter and exit the building because power fluctuations had many expensive appliances that were display models short-circuiting and some burning. The guards had become accustomed to having several repair people coming in many times a week.

The crew had studied the mall for weeks and knew the routine. They knew when electricity went out and when it came back on, and on which specific days of the week. They knew which elevators worked, and which security cameras worked during that time with no electricity. They knew when and how the guards would make rounds. It was easy. They would do it in broad daylight. They knew how to escape undetected. It was so easy.

It was a normal day at the mall. The Mall of Africa had both luxury and cheap stores, the electronics stores and kiosks the most popular. Purposeful shoppers mixed with those who came only to walk around and kill the day. Colette and her two friends left the taxi and joined hundreds of other shoppers in the mall. They had decided that Saturday morning to shop for outdoor gear for their upcoming safari. They dodged a trio of young men, wearing baggy pants and catcalling them, by diverting into a lingerie boutique. After several rounds of different outdoor apparel and fragrance stores, they decided to lunch at the cafeteria. The food was known to be good, and the place was packed.

Colette and her friends got their food and chose a table near the escalators. Joel sat on the next table enjoying his triple cheeseburger while keeping an eye on the girls. Three utility men came to sit at the table near them to enjoy their lunches. One talked on his phone. Colette and her friends took selfies and food pics and posted them to their social media accounts.

It happened as the three men finished their meal and stood up, looking toward Colette and her friends. The blast went off in an instant. The building shook and concrete, boards and brick collapsed. One half of the floor gave way, and then two more floors above it. Shrapnel barreled in every direction. The force from the blast knocked the girls, their chairs, and the table a few meters backwards into the walls. Colette lay still, her body twisted, momentarily dazed. She couldn't breathe. Her ears were blocked and ringing with a whizzing sound. She could hear very faint screams, yelling, people running and falling, thuds as in their panic they collided or tripped on debris. And blood was everywhere. The screams and commotion faded little by little. The last thing she remembered was a masked man in blue overalls carrying her on his shoulders past the stalled escalators full of the frantic masses trying to use them as stairs.

For the three girls, it happened in a flash. Disorienting. Claustrophobic. One moment shopping. One moment an explosion. The next moment being hooded, dragged down to the basement, and being thrown onto the floor of a van.

CHAPTER
ELEVEN

SIX AND REGGIE rented a chalet at a mountain lodge a few kilometers from Mutare. They had woken up at 4:00 a.m. the next morning and taken a 10-km run up the trail to the top of the mountain. Because they were in top shape, this had taken them only forty minutes, while jogging at a talking pace. After they had loaded up on a complimentary English breakfast and showered, they checked out and hit the road towards Chipinge.

They arrived at the private clinic at 10:00. Six asked for his grandmother's hospital bill and paid it with the brick of American cash. A nurse directed them to the room where Grandma Grace was resting. Her left leg was in a cast and propped up on a hook attached to the ceiling. Six and Reggie both hugged her and placed the basket of yellow roses, sunflowers, and pink tulips, with some chocolate truffles, on her nightstand. Grandma Grace was more interested in the truffles.

After exchanging pleasantries, Grandma Grace complained that if she wasn't here, she could have gotten a fire started and cooked for them. Six and

Reggie thanked her and assured her they were already full. She looked a little disappointed but agreed. Food sharing was part of African culture. People liked to eat. When you visited, you ate. There was a local saying that "Blood ties are half the measure; the full measure is realized by eating." Food was the African way.

Despite her insistence on going to the regional hospital, Six had not let his grandmother do that. Public hospitals were understaffed and lacked resources, and dying patients waited in line for hours and hours for a chance to get medication, which was often rationed. The private hospital was expensive, but the service was better.

Reggie's phone rang and she stepped out of the room.

Six said, "What happened, Grandma?"

"I fell. Broke my hip."

"What were you doing?"

"Harvesting maize."

"I told you not to carry fifty-kilogram bags on your head. You're too old—"

"I like work. I'll keep working till I die."

"I gave you money to hire some helping hands with the harvest."

"Yes."

"The doctor said you arrived here two days late."

"I did. I prefer traditional medicine. I don't like the pills from the British."

"Don't tell me you went to the traditional healer."

"I did."

"And did it help?"

"No. But he pulled stuff out of my hip."

"What stuff?"

"Feathers."

Six looked flabbergasted.

"Did he say where they came from?"

"From jealous neighbors, he said. Witchcraft."

Six laughed. "You believe that?"

"I don't know. But we grew up with that stuff."

"Just promise me you will take all the medicine the doctor gives you."

"Don't worry about me. The doc said I'll be out of here soon. The hip surgery went well. It was expensive. I would rather have spent that money in some other way."

"Grandma, don't worry about money. Look at it as having teeth repaired or some necessity like that."

She smiled, exposing a mouth bare of teeth.

"Tell me about Henry," Six said. Henry, Six's cousin, was in jail for stealing seven dollars and some candy at a local kiosk and had been using illegal drugs.

"Oh, Henry," said his grandmother. "Such a waste of potential. Let him be. I think jail time will do him good. He won't have access to drugs in there. So, it's three months of free rehab and hard work. If you can, stop by and chat with him. He will listen to you. He is with the wrong crowd."

"I will."

"What are you going to do when that three months is over?"

"I will get him into a rehab clinic. I've googled a few great ones in Harare. Kids nowadays!"

"That's the consequence of kids who grow up with no purpose. Don't want to work, and expect things handed to them. Too bad that even for the ones who want to work, there are no jobs in this country. Most resort to drugs and alcohol to escape their reality. I'll stop by and see him on my way out."

"I hope that will bring him to his senses."

Six walked to the window.

"Draye Sixpence, are you okay?"

"Yes."

"No, you're not. Come sit here."

Six sat back on the bed next to her.

"Tell me what you are thinking."

"Grandma, I don't know. Sometimes I think I should stay here with you. You're my only relative now. And my job. I keep traveling around while I should be here with you."

Grandma Grace squeezed his hand.

"I'm old and you're young. I've lived a beautiful life. I don't want you to waste your youth on me. Look at all the good you have done around here. For the schools, the children. Thousands and thousands. You can't do any of that while stuck here with me. For what? I'd be selfish if I let you do that. And it's about time you started your own family."

Six remained quiet.

"Listen," she said. "Well-intentioned advice can be bad advice. Use your wisdom and discernment to do what's right for you and those you care about. All else will fall into place."

Reggie came in holding a phone in her hand. She seemed full of urgency.

"Duty calls. We have to be in Vic Falls tomorrow morning."

Reggie glanced from Grandma Grace then to Six.

Grandma Grace smiled, then winked at Six. "You take care of each other, okay?"

Six and Reggie smiled at each other.

"Go on," she said. "I'm in good hands here."

"I'll be back to see you. I'll make sure the doctors take good care of you."

"Thank you, son. Now go!"

"What's up?" Six asked Reggie, while they approached the exit.

"They have found traces of the bomb used for the blast at the Mall of Africa."

"That's a long drive."

"We have all night."

Before they left town, Six retrieved his SIG pistol from his grandmother's grain shack. He always cleaned and buried it in a wooden box in the ground every time he left the country.

CHAPTER
TWELVE

THEY CLIMBED into the Land Cruiser.

"What was the phone call about?" Six said.

"My superiors said they will let me know once we arrive at the station. Those were my only instructions," Reggie said.

"The boss really wanted you with me. The Mall of Africa was bombed. It happened yesterday. And we must act fast. Africa Day is coming."

"Is that important?"

"My boss thinks something bigger is coming."

Six looked out the window. "I don't work for your Bureau."

Reggie unlocked her phone and handed it to Six. "Watch this."

She handed him the phone after unlocking it with face recognition. "Check this out."

Six perused the article about the recent bombing of the Mall of Africa, and played the video, taken by a bystander in a nearby building. Reggie remained quiet while Six watched the horrific explosion without flinching.

"This is crazy! Do they know who did this?"

"Could be extremists. Tribal conflict. We don't know. None of the known groups have claimed responsibility yet."

"I have a few theories."

"Go on."

"All this started off as random acts of isolated terror attacks across four East African countries. But now it has spread to several other countries."

"Countless hate crimes and religious conflicts have been happening for decades."

"But there is no pattern to the attacks. Sometimes it's easy to assess the motivation behind attacks, but these are random. With no economic gain. The last attempt was on the president's motorcade from the showgrounds. He has a lot of enemies from displaced white farmers to his stance on gender issues and abortion. A traditionalist. Considered an enemy from the West, a human rights enemy."

"Your theory is the West is involved?"

"Nothing new. France and Germany have been known to supply guns to rebels. The British and Americans have left trails of discord everywhere: Africa, Asia, Middle East, you name it."

"Divide and conquer."

"Exactly. But the main question is why all these particular places?"

"What do all the attacks and assassinations have in common?"

"Zero," Reggie said. "Looks random to me. East, west, north, south, and central Africa, seven attacks, all in the last few months."

Six thought for a second. "There has to be some connection."

"Maybe."

"Three events involved prominent politicians."

"Yes, but the other four did not. A church congregation. A soccer match. A mall. A mosque. A national bank. A youth rally—"

"Any reason. The wrong word. The cancel culture and political correctness of today. You anger people without even knowing."

"People are so sensitive nowadays," Reggie said.

"I get that on attacking politicians, but why churches, malls, and rallies?"

"Could be anything. Mental illness."

"These weren't done by one mentally ill person. Could be a distraction. Maybe they've planned a bigger attack on Africa Day. How many victims?"

"Thirty casualties. Women, men, and children. Your personal hypothesis?"

"Terrorism. Tribal wars have been increasing over East Africa. Now with more religious extremists rampant in the area, ISIS has been reported to have small bases there."

"Well, that's a needle in a haystack."

"Let me check with my contact," said Six. "Might have some intel for us."

"Thank you."

"Don't thank me yet," Six said. "If this thing is worse than random, as you're saying, then I've a feeling this will require a hell of a lot more resources and time."

"Our intelligence shows that."

"But why involve me?"

"The Director wants you!"

"Which Director?"

"Of AULEB."

"He isn't my director. Not my problem."

"But isn't this what you always wanted?"

"I don't work for your Bureau."

"I'm putting together a team. He learned what we did last time, and he wanted us to do it again. Doesn't trust anyone."

"If I say no?"

"I'll have to hunt you down."

"My second theory is that it comes more from the outside. A Pan-Africanist activist was gunned down in Addis Ababa in broad daylight while on a train station. And we suspect there is more. Spies, operatives, working to eliminate leaders of the movement."

"From?"

"Could be The CIA, MI6, the French or Chinese intelligence agencies," said Reggie.

"Maybe a terrorist cell."

"It's too many events in too short a time to be a small group. Look," said Reggie, handing Six her phone. "That's another victim."

"Who is he?"

"A prominent member of the AU Security Council. Assassinated at a lodge in Victoria Falls two days ago."

"These may not be connected," Six said. "The mall was clearly a massacre. Open terrorism. This one was a targeted assassination."

"But they all happened the same day. What are the odds? My boss said higher-ups wanted help finding who killed this guy, and if it's all connected to the bombings. We believe he was meeting someone in Vic Falls, the guy killed in the lodge. My team reviewed footage from the lodge's hallway and lobby cameras of all the occupants staying that night. The man is seen arriving with a woman, and she leaves three hours later."

"Having an affair, possibly."

"We questioned the woman in the video, but she was innocent. She's just a local college girl who makes money that way. We interviewed all the guests and staff, but no success."

"What else do we know about the victim?"

"Checked phone records, emails, social media. We combed through any possible online footprint. Clean. The last call he made was to his wife."

"It's possible our person of interest might be using another form of communication. Was it a diplomatic visit?"

"No. His office says there wasn't any scheduled on his calendar."

"Why would a high-profile political figure just travel across the continent with no security like that?"

"Doesn't add up. Was he doing illegal stuff? Corruption, trafficking, or stuff like that, that he didn't want anyone to know?"

"And we are to find who's doing this?"

"The agency thinks it's an organized crime ring. There must be a leader somewhere who is orchestrating the weapons supply, transport, and cash."

"That's going to be a pain in the ass. Where do we start? It's not like these guys will leave emails or anything trackable."

"That's the thing. Unlike other extremist groups like ISIS, no one is claiming these mass murders. But criminals eventually make mistakes." Reggie paused and then said, "Your agency has resources we don't have."

"I've to convince the boss first. I don't create

missions. They are usually handed to me, and I follow orders."

"All we're asking is you do your best."

Six thought for a minute.

"You have jurisdiction across all countries in Africa," Six said.

"We do."

That opened up a lot of possibilities.

CHAPTER
THIRTEEN

THE BLACK HOOD came off and Colette adjusted her eyes. Her head hurt as if it had been split. She felt the dried blood on the back of her head. Colette noticed she was in a sprinter cargo van. No seats. No windows. She hated confined spaces. The only light came from the front.

Two men sat in the front seats behind the wire mesh that separated them from the cargo area. There were letters printed on the backs of their overalls of what looked like a company logo. Colette couldn't move her arms. Her hands had been raised slightly above her head and were tied to the van rails. They were painful, and worse was her whole body jolting from the constant bumps in the road. She sensed her friend, Judith, tossing and twisting beside her. She tapped Judith's foot with her leg. Judith seemed to understand this and stopped fidgeting.

Colette strained her eyes to see who might have pulled off her hood. There was a dark silhouette in the shadow of the rear of the van. It was a man.

She could hear him breathing. Colette did not make a sound. She noticed another man bound on the van's floor motionless. *Joel!*

Colette had watched child-trafficking documentary films and their images played in her mind. *Is this what was happening?* she thought. *Are we going to die? Be sold into prostitution? Never see our parents again*? Using her foot, Colette felt around for her other friend, Priscilla. Priscilla tapped her foot back. No one made any sound. Colette wanted her friends free. She had convinced them to come shopping. She knew her dad would move heaven and earth to seek her out. But when and how?

The man in the passenger seat phoned someone. Colette listened.

"Boss, we have the package. Out of the country now."

"Perfect."

"We are three hours out."

"Good. Make sure they get here untouched."

Colette's father Chris had taught her safety lessons, because being from a wealthy family might tempt kidnappers. It was always a possibility. More and more people loathed the wealthy. Colette tried to feel where her phone was on her body. Her phone was gone. Colette remembered that her Apple watch could place emergency calls if she could hold the power button. She twisted her bound wrists and pressed the power button against the railing. A few seconds later her screen lit up, illuminating the van. Her heart jumped. And the call went through.

Flushed with her small victory, Colette did not

see the man until his massive hand gripped her wrist.

"What do we have here?"

Colette tried shaking off his grip. He twisted her wrist so that the rope cut into her skin. It hurt like hell. He undid the Apple Watch.

The heavily bearded captor put his face close to Colette's. "You smartass. No one will find you here. By the time the police get here, you'll be where they will never find you."

His comrades in the front, having seen the watch's light, slammed on the brakes, skidding onto an embankment. The back van doors swung open, and the three men, all brandishing guns, searched the girls. They took their fitness trackers and wallets and watches.

One planted his gun on Colette's temple.

"You are lucky the boss wants you untouched. You know what I would do to you? Don't do something stupid like that again!"

"Looks like her SOS call went through."

"We'd better hit the road fast."

"Should we tell the boss?"

"No! You know what he will do to us."

"Then what should we do with these?"

"Destroy them."

They crushed the fitness trackers and watches and dumped them into the tall grass on the side of the road. The van screeched back onto the road and sped off.

When the van doors swung open again, it was night. The three girls were dragged over some grass onto a narrow gravel strip. There were no buildings in sight. The only light was from the moon, the van's headlights, and the small plane a few yards ahead. They were loaded into an old Soviet biplane, an Antonov An-2, on an airstrip in the middle of nowhere. The plane took off shortly.

CHAPTER
FOURTEEN

THIS YEAR, Sheila's fundraising gala was held at the couple's penthouse in Sandton, a suburb in the Johannesburg metropolitan area, and just one of the many properties the couple owned across Africa. This was the only time in the year they used this place unless Chris had a meeting in Joburg or a family function. The gala was held annually to raise money for the Chris and Sheila Osage Foundation local pregnancy centers.

The lavish annual event had to be held in Joburg, because that was where the big donors were. Chris hated these events, but he went anyway. He had come to understand all the fake smiles rich people gave each other while judging who wore what by which designer. He preferred to spend his time chasing the world, building a legacy for the whole continent. From the floor-to-ceiling windows of the penthouse, on the fortieth floor, he could see all the way to Soweto. Just a few blocks away were shacks full of otherwise homeless people. Johannesburg was an interesting city, a tango between the haves and have-nots, the old and new, whites, blacks, and every shade in be-tween; those on top, and those at the bottom; a bleak past and a hopeful future. Chris and Sheila were part of that hope. Hope for Colette, and thousands of other young people.

The sliding glass walls opened to the expansive rooftop garden. A local D.J. played jazz in the background.

The invited guests started arriving at 6:30. Sheila and Chris greeted each one of them at the elevators that opened into their penthouse. The caterers served drinks and food at various standing and sitting tables spread indoors and in the rooftop garden. Colette had been excused from the event, being busy preparing for her upcoming trip. Among the guests were South Africa's elite and a few from outside of the country including politicians, business tycoons, educators, and musicians. The women wore elegant dresses, and the men flamboyant dark tuxedos and hats of all sizes, styles, shapes, and designs.

Assorted cheeses, charcuterie, seafood bites, and *biltong*—a favorite local specialty—accompanied the cocktails and assorted specialty wines from local vineyards in the Western Cape. This was followed by a steak dinner at 8:00. Several stations had items displayed for silent auction, including crafts made by women at the local pregnancy center, and items donated by the locals which included rare Chinese porcelains, ceramics, sculptures, and a few first-edition books, old-time classics.

At 8:30 p.m. Sheila brought the place to order. She thanked the guests for their continued support for the Osage Foundation and the local pregnancy centers where their generosity had improved the lives of hundreds of women and children. Lastly, she encouraged the guests to enjoy the food and drink.

On several TV and podcast interviews, Chris had mentioned, indirectly, the idea of running for president, whether in this election cycle or the next. Chris had been elected Chairman of the African Union Economic Development Fund. He was chairman of the board for the Africa Railway Commission, tasked to oversee the Cape-to-Cairo speed-rail project. The railroad's completion would connect the continent and facilitate efficient transport of goods and people all the way from South Africa to Egypt. The mega project was to bring over fifty billion dollars across the continent and over ten million jobs over the next four years. Proposals for the project came from Anglo-American companies, German companies, Chinese companies, and even Japanese. Often the proposals came with bribes and promises of kickbacks.

Two men in black suits slid into chairs in front of Chris. They removed and sat their dark fedoras on their laps. They shook hands.

"Mr. Osage, I'm Steve. This is my colleague, John."

"You do have last names?"

"We are representing an Anglo-American client with vested interest in the railway project. Starting in this country."

Chris sized up the two men. They had been drinking; they were not serious. He was used to pitches, in person or by mail. It was common for strangers, wanna-be entrepreneurs, to pitch their big ideas to him for a small investment of only a hundred thousand dollars. Most made their pitches at inopportune times. Politicians, presidents of non-profits; he had heard from them all. All vying for donations for their big campaigns. The truth is, Chris rarely paid attention to these pitches or the written proposals. He had a whole team he paid for that task. His only role was to give final approval and sign the checks.

His bodyguards approached to apprehend the men. Chris waved them off.

"This is a great thing your family is doing here," the one named Steve, said.

"That's nice of you. Now what can I do for you, Steve and John?"

"You and we both know that if you run for office you don't have a chance to win against the ANC or other established parties."

"I don't even know if it's worth it."

Steve continued, "The point is, those parties have a stronghold in this country. Even if the leaders feed them shit, people will still vote for them."

"That's politics, I suppose."

"With us on your side, the presidency could be yours. We can make things happen. And more profits will come after the railway is complete. Every type of goods will be transported through it. We know you're not stupid. You can see the writing on the wall."

"What you say is true. But what kind of man would I be if I betray my values?"

"Values? They all say that at the beginning, before they taste power."

"But I'm not them. My character is what keeps me going. The day I start taking bribes is the day I no longer belong. And I'm going to be the difference. We all die one day or another. None of us are remembered for the riches we had, but the impact we had on others."

Steve leaned back into his chair.

"Correct to an extent. But don't you want to live knowing that your children and their children don't have to worry about money ever again?"

"I have all the money I need. Even if I didn't, at what expense? Hundreds of millions of my people?"

"Life is not fair. Not everyone wins."

"Gentlemen, your time is almost up."

"Either way, the Chinese will be bad news for the continent. History repeats itself. The continent might not be yours in a few decades. Don't you want secure property rights and wealth for your children and grandchildren?"

"What good is it to choose one evil over another evil?"

"One is a lesser evil."

"My position on this remains unchanged. I will only approve the proposal that's good for my people, not outside interests."

The two men stood.

"Well, thank you for your time, Mr. Osage."

Steve left a card on the table. No name, just a phone number. They slid their hats on and stood and took the elevator.

CHRIS'S PHONE RANG. It was Joel, Colette's bodyguard.

Chris moved to a quieter space and answered. "Here?" he said.

"We've got your daughter!" the deep, electronically enhanced voice said.

The words felt like a rock placed on Chris's chest. Suffocating. Yet at the same time his heart was pounding its way out of his chest. Chris composed himself but did not respond.

"We've got you daughter, you bastard!"

"Where's Joel?"

Joel's frantic voice yelled from the background, "Sir, they have—they have her! They—" He was cut short by the sound of a gunshot.

"Who are you and what do you want? Money?"

The man on the other side laughed hysterically. "To you it's all money, money. Not everything is about money!"

"Then what do you want?"

"You will get instructions on how to get your daughter back on this number. If you make a stupid move, she dies. Understand?"

"Understood. Please don't harm my daughter!" Chris said.

"Her life depends on the moves you make next. It's all in your hands. Do anything stupid, she will end up like her bodyguard."

The call ended. Chris dropped the mobile phone onto the table. His armpits and palms sweated. His knees felt weak. He feigned a smile as his wife approached.

"Is everything okay, honey?" said Sheila, who had been watching her husband.

"Honey, something came up at work. Not worth worrying about."

"Who were those two men?"

"Some businesspeople talking business."

"I told you, no business today."

"I can't control who comes to talk to me."

Sheila smiled. "Come on. Let's go mingle with our guests. I know you don't like small talk with a lot of people, but do it just this one day, for me."

Chris kissed her on the forehead.

Sheila hooked her husband's hand in hers and they walked into the terrace garden.

Having been married to Chris for seventeen years, Sheila knew when Chris was distraught and that he would try not to show it. She knew his ups and downs as a businessman. There were some things that Chris would not tell her even if he wanted to. She also knew not to embarrass him in public. But she could sense his discomfort. Something was not right.

He excused himself.

"Honey?" Sheila said.

Chris furrowed his brow and said, "I need to call my head of security."

"Can he fix whatever is wrong?"

"Just trying to make sure my trip to Addis Ababa is good to go."

"You're not okay. I have never seen you sweat this much. Are you getting sick?"

Chris didn't answer. Without looking at his wife, Chris entered his office and locked the door behind himself. Inside the office, Chris cried. He had made tough decisions before, such as firing employees, but this was a different level of pain. He could kill for his daughter. He offered a silent prayer. Then he felt rage he had never felt before. He took a few deep controlled breaths, wiped his eyes, and picked up the phone. It rang only once.

"Yes, boss."

"Tali, get your man ready here in five minutes."

"Yes, boss!"

Chris explained the situation to Tali. Tali and some of his security staff were on the third floor of the high-rise, in a surveillance room, where they monitored the entire building and the penthouse while Chris was in town.

Chris composed himself and went back to the terrace. Sheila smiled at him. He forced a smile back and accepted a drink. Chris spent the rest of the night going through the motions, shaking hands, trying to remain calm, but the truth is his mind was not there. He was counting down the clock until the time when the gala would end.

CHAPTER
FIFTEEN

STEVE AND JOHN staggered from the elevator to their BMW sedan in the building's underground garage. They had primed themselves with too many cocktails. Little did they notice the occupants of two black Escalade SUVs parked twenty feet from them were watching. Steve got into the driver's seat and fumbled with engine's start button. The sedan backed up and wound through the garage up to the surface street. They turned on loud rock-and-roll music. The black Escalades followed right out behind them. A mile later, the sedan merged onto the M75 freeway towards the Johannesburg metro area, and so did the two black SUVs.

The two men decided to stop to use a restroom. They exited the highway and parked at a convenience store. They used the restroom, and walked back to the car. There were two black SUVs parked on either side of their BMW. The two drunks didn't care until several men grabbed each one of them while muffling any sound they might with a swift application of duct tape. Steve and John had their phones taken, were hooded, then thrown separately into the two black SUVs where their hands and feet were bound. They were both still in shock. Armed carjackings in Joburg did happen, some even in broad daylight. But now they had been kidnapped. The two SUVs backed out and merged into the highway.

The SUVs drove past Soweto Township, then turned right onto a single-lane road for a kilometer, then slowed down, turning left onto a gravel road that led, after about forty-five minutes, to an apple farm northeast of the township. The gravel road led to a log cabin that was used as a safe house by Chris and his team, a stone's throw from the main house. Chris came here with his friends during hunting season. He owned the 12,000-hectare farm.

The SUVs parked in front of the safe house. Tali and his men dragged the two hooded men in. Both men were strapped to metal chairs in separate rooms.

The thin walls ensured Steve could hear all of John's screams as he was being interrogated. They used this to play the two men. Steve heard all the wailing and knew John was being tortured. Steve panicked and wet his pants. The buzz from the booze was gone. John screamed and screamed, then was quiet. Steve trembled. Moments later he heard footfalls approaching his room. The door opened, then several people walked in. Two men helped lift his hood partway up. He could see the interrogators in silhouette behind the lights, but couldn't see their faces. The hood was removed and a bright LED floodlight blasted directly into his face. Steve winced as the light hit his eyes, causing pain and temporary blindness. That amount of concentrated light was enough to fry a retina.

Tali walked around and pulled Steve's head backwards by the hair and talked into his ear. "This is going to be fun. Looks like you already pissed your pants!"

Steve was trembling so hard they could hear his teeth chattering.

"Who put you up to this?" one of his tormentors said.

"What...What are you talking about?"

"The girl."

"What girl!? I have no idea what you are talking about. What—?"

A backhanded slap caught Steve off guard. Then a fist from the right caught him in the jaw before he could process the first hit. He spit blood and a tooth out. Blood trickled down the corner of his mouth onto his white shirt.

Steve cried, "I don't know what this is about."

Tali spoke. "Look, we can do this the hard way or the easy way. Your choice. We have all night."

One of Tali's men rolled a cart into the room. On the cart was a tray with knives, pliers, scissors, and jumper cables. Steve saw the shiny knife blade. A bucket of water was placed beside Steve.

Steve pleaded, "Please, can you at least tell me what this is about?"

The man showed them a picture. "You recognize this girl?"

"No. Who is she?"

"The girl your people kidnapped!"

"Oh God. Kidnapping? Why would we kidnap someone?"

He received a fist to the stomach, right above

the liver, and coughed sputum and blood. The pain shot through Steve's spine. For a moment he thought his body would shut down from the pain. Blood ran from his mouth and nose, staining the white dress shirt.

Steve gagged, and spoke heavily, "I've never met that girl. Is she dead?" He paused seeking a response from his interrogators. "Oh, God. Why me?"

Tali placed his hand on Steve's shoulder.

"Calm down. We are just getting started. What happened to the girl? Okay, I'm going to pretend you don't know about this girl. She was kidnapped earlier this evening."

"I have an alibi. I was at the gala. You can check with the host. Check through my phone. I can give you my passcode and you can see all the messages, phone calls, and emails I have sent or received this year. You can ask my girlfriend as well."

Tali's man exported details from Steve's phone.

"Did you hear about a kidnapping, a teenaged girl?"

"No. I'm a business consultant. I'd never get involved with stuff like that. I have two sisters and a mother, okay?"

Tali left the room and phoned Chris.

"Boss, I don't think these guys did it. With all we did to them, they should have admitted it. Checked all their phone records. Clean."

"Are you sure?"

"Yes, boss. This is what I do. Probably wrong place at the wrong time."

Chris sighed. "You can let them go."

Tali returned to the room and had the two men untied from the chairs. They were hooded and carried into a black SUV. Forty-five minutes later, the cars stopped. The two men were dragged out for a distance and their hands unbound. They were ordered to kneel in the grass, hands behind their heads. Guns were placed behind their hooded heads.

Tali said, "Give me a reason to not blow your brains out right now."

"Please! We have already told you."

"If I let you two go, will you utter a word of what happened today to anyone?"

"Never," Steve said. "Not me!"

"Not me," John said.

"I know where you live and work. I also know where your families are. If I ever hear any of this in the media, I'll kill each and every one of them and you, last. What will you say if someone asks you what happened to you?"

Steve spoke. "An accident. I fell and hit a post."

"I work from home, so I won't go out until I'm healed," John said.

The two men kept on talking, trying to provide convincing ways they were going to avoid any suspicion from neighbors and coworkers. There was silence, then the vehicle roared away. John was the first to emerge from his daze, and slowly lifted his hood.

"Steve! They are gone!"

They had been abandoned somewhere off the highway, where they could see the traffic zooming by in the distance. Their BMW was there. The Escalade had already disappeared into the highway. The two men looked at each other, incredulous.

They embraced and staggered into the car.

CHAPTER
SIXTEEN

THE NEXT FEW hours of the night were painful for Chris and Sheila, especially Sheila. They phoned the parents of Colette's two friends and learned they were also missing. The families vowed to remain quiet until Chris solved the matter, and offered any help they could. The next morning the two families came to Chris and Sheila's penthouse, talked, and then left. They all felt helpless.

Chris recalled every detail of the bone-chilling phone call to his wife. They locked the Joburg penthouse and jetted back to Cape Town. Their driver dropped them at their mansion in Clifton, a suburb overlooking the Atlantic Ocean. Sheila wailed all the way there, asking "What if she's hurt? "What if they kill her? Oh, I couldn't live!" and a hundred other awful speculations, and had not stopped crying. Chris did his best to console her, but there was little he could do. He assured her he would do all in his power to get their daughter back. She blamed him, snarled at him, then prayed. He couldn't blame her; he felt the pain too. But he had to be strong for her—and for their daughter.

The two stayed on the couch in their living room all day and evening, while Chris waited and hoped for another call. Sheila cried herself to exhaustion. Chris eventually stood up and poured himself a glass of whiskey. It was past 11:00 p.m., his usual bedtime, but he couldn't sleep. He knew he would never be able to sleep for the next few days. Not until he got his baby back. The Steve and John route had turned out to be a dead end. *So, who did this?* He knew he had enemies, but struggled to guess which one would be capable of grabbing his daughter from a mall and taking her God knows where. He walked out the glass doors to the patio overlooking the beach. The waves and sound seemed to calm him.

His phone rang. It was from the head of his security team.

"Tali," Chris said.

"Sir, we found something."

"Okay. I'm on my way."

Before leaving, Chris ordered the house aides to keep an eye on Sheila and make sure she didn't hurt herself. And to bring her whatever she needed and to phone him when she woke up and needed him.

Chris met with his security detail in the cottage on the south side of the property. This was the team's home base, staffed 24/7. Tali led Chris to a room equipped with state-of-the-art security features, spyware, computers, live video feeds. There were eight other team members in the room, four of them on computers.

The team had detected the location of Colette's

Apple watch, just across the Mozambique-South Africa border. They had also traced an SOS call attempt from her watch at 1500 hours, a few miles away in the same area.

"I want people there," Chris barked. "I want them found. Ask everyone you can."

"Yes, sir!"

They tapped Chris's phone and they waited for the next call from the kidnappers to see if they could track it, while three loaded Escalades and a chopper were dispatched from Chris's fleet to search for Colette.

Chris turned to the head of security. "Any updates on the delegate?"

"His itinerary is confirmed. He agreed to meet you in Addis Ababa on Thursday."

"That's in two days."

"Yes, sir."

"Connect me to the director of the Bureau."

Tali dialed a few numbers on the secure line, then waited.

"Sir, the director is on line two."

Chris picked the receiver. The phone beeped twice.

The voice from the other end said, "Chris! For what do I have the pleasure of speaking to my old friend this late?"

"They took her, Gerald. They have my daughter! They have Colette!"

Chris heard bedsheets rustle as Gerald sat up in bed.

Gerald Shiri was the Director for the African Union Intelligence and Law Enforcement Bureau, AULEB. Gerald and Chris had met while Gerald was a detective and helped Chris solve an extortion case about a decade ago. The two men had become friends. Gerald was good at his job fighting corruption, and he had climbed the ranks to police commissioner of Johannesburg. Previously he had led the counter-terrorism center in Addis Ababa, Ethiopia, established to quell severe religious extremist bombings across the continent. When Chris lobbied for the formation of a law enforcement agency with overarching powers across the continent, Gerald supported him. When the AU Security Council approved the formation of the agency, Gerald was hired as the first director. Chris paid twenty million dollars for the construction of the headquarters.

Chris sobbed. "They have her, Gerald! And two other girls."

Gerald was now up pacing in his kitchen.

"They called," said Chris, "and said they will call again with instructions."

"Did they say what they wanted?"

"No. I know nothing so far."

"I'm setting my guys on this right now!"

"Thanks, Gerald."

"We will get her back. Make sure you take care of yourself for now."

CHAPTER
SEVENTEEN

ON THEIR WAY FROM CHIPINGE, Six and
Reggie decided to take a detour on their way to Vic
Falls. They figured they would still arrive around
midnight to early morning. Six wanted to see an
old foe. They took the roundabout just before
Gweru and headed towards Harare. About forty
kilometers north, they got off Highway A17 towards the Hwahwa maximum-security prison.
Hwahwa was Zimbabwe's second-most-ruthless
prison, reserved for people who had been convicted of treason, murder, and other heinous acts
that were beyond sane human comprehension. The
prison had been the home for some of the nation's
most notorious murderers, robbers, and prisoners
of war during the guerrilla warfare with the
Rhodesian forces prior to independence. Reggie
and Six barreled through a freshly smoothed
gravel road towards the prison, over a stretch of
empty woodlands and savannah. The end of the
trail was a mixture of gravel, sand, and red loam.

They saw the guard tower first over the trees,
then saw the outer perimeter three-meter fence.

Reggie showed her badge to the two armed guards at the gate. Six did likewise. Asked what their business here was, they spoke briefly. The car was searched, and two German shepherds sniffed around the car. Satisfied, the guards let them through towards the inner security perimeter. This was an eight-foot-high brick wall, twelve inches thick, with coiled razor wire on top. This gate had several more guards in a security hut. These guards performed the same procedures, handling the badges, doing searches, and more German shepherds sniffed through the car. Six and Reggie had to surrender their handguns. One guard directed them to the parking lot, and told them how to get to the entrance and visiting area.

They passed a group of prisoners working in the garden. The guard at the entrance asked whom they were here to see. They stated their business.

The sun was then setting. Crimson horizon. Beautiful African sun over the savannah.

There were two guards in the office: a man and a woman.

The man spoke through the little window.

"What's your business?"

"Here to see Mayor Hove."

The guard eyed them up and down.

"I.D.s?"

They both handed their I.D.s. He put the I.D.s into a receptacle and into a locker. He then called his colleague to get Mayor Hove for a visit.

"You're lucky," the woman said. "Visitation time has only fifteen minutes left. We don't let people in after visiting hours."

"This way," the man said.

He led Six and Reggie to the visitation area. It

had concrete benches on one side, a thick plastic barrier between, and another concrete seating block on the other side. Small holes in the plastic barricade could transmit voices and sound, but they were not big enough for anything else.

"Wait here. He will be here shortly."

Six and Reggie waited.

A few minutes later the iron door opened. Mayor Hove entered behind a guard. He was led to the concrete block. He looked disheveled, unkempt, with stubble on his chin. He wore handcuffs and flip-flops and an orange jumpsuit with the Roman numerals MIV on his back—his inmate ID number. He had lost weight since the last time they had seen him. Hove now had protruding cheekbones and sunken eyes. Other than that, he looked okay. His jumpsuit looked clean and pressed. The guard stood, back to the wall, keeping an eye on the interaction.

When he noticed Six and Reggie on the other side of the barrier Hove forced a sarcastic grin, exposing teeth yellowed from years of whiskey and tobacco.

"Well, well, well. To what pleasure do I have to receive such visitors?"

"Surprise," Six said. "Your handymen failed to put me down."

Hove's eyes widened. "What are you talking about?"

"You sent your cronies to kill me, but they failed."

"Okay, you survived, so what? Did you just come here to brag that you survived? It's jail. People fight and kill each other all the time."

"I know you are still part of the crime ring

selling drugs. And you have many cops in your pocket. Are your guys still selling Triple Z?"

"How can I be running drugs outside?" said Hove. He lifted his handcuffed hands. Then smiled his awful smile. "Detective Kona, and Six. You are good at this; the best. In fact the best. You will figure it out. And when you do, I'll be here."

"We will," Reggie said. "And I'll make sure you never leave this place until your sorry old ass is dead!"

Mayor Hove laughed mockingly.

"We shall see," he said, pointing to the wall clock. Time is moving. Looks like our time is up. Good to be catching up with old friends."

"I hate bullies," Reggie said.

Hove stood up and yelled, "Guard. We are done here!" As the guard led him away, Hove said, "There are more important things to worry about, my friends. The big event is coming. Something is in the air. You hear me, the time is coming up! Tick-tock, tick-tock." He stared back at them, an insidious grin on his aging face, until the iron door closed behind him.

They left the prison just after sundown. In seven hours, they would be in Vic Falls, if they drove 140 kilometers per hour. Six drove. He liked to drive.

CRIME and illegal drug deaths had dropped drastically since the new Vic Falls police chief replaced the old police chief whom Six and Reggie had helped put behind bars months earlier.

After visiting the Vic Falls police station to get

updates on the current homicide victim, Six and Reggie went to the regional hospital's morgue to see the medical examiner.

They found Joyce at the lab hunched over the body with a headlamp and a magnifying glass. Joyce was a forensics scientist and medical examiner at the Vic Falls Regional Hospital. She had worked with Six and Reggie to solve several murders months earlier.

The victim's body was on a cart, covered with a white sheet except for his head. His face was bashed in.

Joyce lifted the magnifying glass she was using and looked up. "Look who's here. Hello, stranger."

"Hi, Joyce," Six said.

"Hi, handsome. I'd have bet you had abandoned this place."

"I like this place."

"I still want my coffee as promised."

"I know."

Reggie and Six put on some latex gloves. Joyce waved them to the examination table where the body was lying.

"What's the cause of death?" Six said.

"Still haven't found the exact cause. Possible homicide. But we don't know the motivation."

"Drug dealing?"

"Possible. Possibly gang-related," Reggie said. "Kids are increasingly getting access to illegal firearms here. And with the drug trade increasing for Triple Z, there have been several murders not just in Vic Falls, but across the country. But all of the drug deaths were of age twenty-five and below."

Triple Z was an illegal drug that had been rampant, despite crackdowns by the police across the country.

Joyce handed Reggie the medical report.

"Forced asphyxiation? A violent crime," Joyce said. "Whoever did it wasn't trying to hide the homicide. That's for sure."

"Drugs?"

"Same. Triple Z."

"A targeted attack," Reggie said. "I still think it's gang related. Nothing was stolen from him or the room."

"Was the guy seeing prostitutes? The report says they found high levels of Triple Z and used condoms in the trash can. Someone leaked the information, and the press are having a field day with the story."

"CCTV footage from the hotel we reviewed showed him arriving with a girl. She left around 9:00 p.m."

"Doesn't align," Joyce said. "He died around 11:00 p.m."

"Which aligns with what the girl told detectives," Reggie said.

"No credentials on him when he was found."

They thanked Joyce and left.

They stayed at Reggie's two-bedroom apartment that she now rented in downtown Victoria Falls.

CHAPTER
EIGHTEEN

KARIM FINISHED SNORTING Triple Z in the bathroom. He went through the ritual, smacking the back of his head while looking up. His pupils dilated. Ah, euphoric! He had found that a slap to the back of his head made the powder hit just the right spot. This was from the recent batch delivered to Vic Falls. He knew the drug was bad for him. It was one reason his wife became cold to him. He felt good after each snort. Superman for a short while, then guilt afterwards. He was convinced he was addicted to it now—sometimes in the morning, mid-morning, afternoon, now even at midnight. Several hours without the substance was torture: intense fever-like symptoms, anxiety, and irritability. Inability to concentrate. He vowed he would quit someday. He put his glasses back on and looked at his reflection in the bathroom mirror and thought, *Who am I kidding?*

Karim returned and sat at the coffee bar. He ordered a latte and French toast.

His phone buzzed.

"Merchandise arrived okay?" the drawling French voice said.

"Yes, Father."

"I have my guys collecting it as we speak. It's already out."

"Good. Did the girls arrive?"

"Yes," the voice said. "I still need that document. Chris is hard-headed. He won't hand over that document easy. I know he is going to try to make some stupid move."

"But for his daughter—?"

"I care less about them. That document means the whole world to me. You understand, don't you, son?"

"Yes, Father."

"Let's not leave anything to chance."

"My people are working on finding the next target. We have some information from inside."

"You trust this info? You failed me last time," the voice said. "Don't fail me again."

Karim paused. Sometimes he contemplated putting a bullet into the old man's head and ending his misery. "Yes, Father. I won't let you down."

The call ended.

Karim stared across the coffee bar. The buzz from the drug tended to cause him to see the material world in a funny way. He thought about this while listening to the baristas talking across the counter.

"Do you call it 'milk' or 'melk'?" one of the female baristas said.

"Melk," another replied.

"Semantics," yet another one replied.

"In America, yes. It's 'melk,'" she said.

"The British pronounce it 'milk.'"

Karim's brow furrowed. He shook his head at the purposelessness of this generation. He was thankful when their voices faded as a duo started to play. A man and a woman. A piano and a harp. A kind of old-school jazz, with an East Asian touch to it. The music was good. The café patrons gave them loud and long applause.

With effort, Karim shifted his focus to across the room.

<hr>

IN LATE AFTERNOON, Reggie decided to stop by the local coffee shop along Main Street, three blocks from the Victoria Falls police station, to go over the reports. Unbeknownst to Reggie, one man was watching her from a table near the pastry bar. She didn't bother asking Six to come along, since he was now staying at the Safari Club.

Reggie observed only the three men across the bar who were watching her too. Another man came in and joined them. He took off his jacket and sat at the counter with them. There seemed to be a spat between the three men and the other one who had just come in. Moments later she watched the three men drag the fourth guy out of the bar. Reggie debated whether to go after them to investigate. She followed them.

She met Six down the street.

"What are you doing out here this late?" she said.

"Fresh air," Six said. "You? I didn't know you drank."

"I don't. Had to clear my head and do some research."

"Have you?"

Reggie nodded her head toward to the direction that led to the alley, where there was a shade used for treading tobacco bales.

"Your target?"

"Yes, my hunch tells me we might get a lead from these guys. I'm on a trail."

"Let's go."

Six and Reggie hooked hands and followed down the street.

"Whatcha got?"

"Drug dealers. Three potential bagmen here to collect dues. Probably just unemployed young men promised a payday if they eliminate a distraction."

They caught up with the four men in the alley. The three men were surrounding one guy who was writhing on the ground.

"Where is our money?" The leader said, kicking the downed man in the stomach.

"Let him go!" Reggie said.

The three men looked back, surprised.

"Lady, you are in the wrong place," the leader said. "Go on your way and mind your own business."

He pulled up his oversized t-shirt to reveal an unholstered revolver in his waistband as he said this.

Six stepped forward. Reggie held him back and said, "I got this."

Six nodded, and stepped back to the side at an angle that gave him an advantage if he needed to step in.

"Who sent you?" Reggie said.

"Why should we tell you? Go on your way if you want to live. This has nothing to do with you."

"My conscience can't let me leave while you kill someone."

"Not your business."

"I will give you a chance, boys, to let the man go, and I will be on my way."

"And if we refuse?" another man said, brandishing a knife he had strapped to his belt.

"There is only one way to find out."

"Big mistake, lady."

Six took his phone and started recording.

"Bitch!" One man charged, swinging his arms. Reggie sidestepped and stiff-armed him into a brick wall.

The men lunged at Reggie and Six. Reggie scooped the first man from under his feet while at the same time removing the gun from his waistband. She threw it towards Six. The man crashed to the ground. His friends came at Reggie; the man with the knife approached her first. Reggie stood firm as the man pressed forward, holding his knife out, making wide arches, side to side. Easy! She did a double reverse kick, catching the man's midsection. Action and reaction. The force jerked the man backwards, disarming him. He fell to the ground groaning. She turned to the third man just as he swung for her head. She dodged to the side and, using the man's momentum, grabbed his left arm, swooped and slammed the man to the ground. He grabbed her jacket and tried to bite Reggie's arm. She pinned his head to the ground with her foot and twisted his left arm some more until the man's face was planted in dirt. He yelped. He let go of her clothes.

"Who paid you?"

"He paid us to do it. The man at the café!"

"I asked who?"

"The guy wearing glasses!"

She twisted some more. "Does this man have a name?"

"How should I know, lady? He just paid us, okay!"

Reggie looked hard at the man's face.

She let go of his arm and again shoved his face into the ground with her boot. The man limped away as fast as he could, leaving the backpack behind. It was loaded with Triple Z bricks.

"These kids know nothing. Bunch of junkies. Let's go."

They looked at the man who had been beaten, who had worked his way up to a sitting position and was leaning on the wall.

Reggie said, "Get a job. Your life is way better than this. Here is a card, take it to the hospital and get treated. I don't want to ever see you out here again, understand?"

"Yes, ma'am!" He staggered away, got his bearings, and fled.

Six replayed the recording on his phone.

"That was pretty good, partner."

"They were just college kids."

"Still."

"That's why sometimes I think we should raise kids on farms. They learn responsibility and self-reliance. Did you like growing up on a farm?"

Six paused, reminiscing. He had helped at a small ranch near his hometown in Oklahoma City which his parents owned. That was many summers ago before he left for college. His parents had always encouraged him to while they were alive. He smiled.

"Yes and no. Unless you are Amish, I doubt those people on the farms want to raise their kids that way. It's just an outcome of circumstances."

"But it gives a better perspective on life. You realize that no one is coming to save you. Being a farmer, if you don't work, you don't eat."

"I agree."

CHAPTER
NINETEEN

ON THE WAY to the station to meet with Reggie's superiors, Six's phone sizzled, showing an incoming message. His phone had been cold for a while.

An incoming message notification lit up the screen. This was the first encrypted message since his last mission in Victoria Falls a few months earlier. He stopped and entered a password to unlock the message.

The message read: *Important new client. Addis Ababa. 12 p.m. Tomorrow. Instructions to follow.*

"What's that?" Reggie said.

He sighed. "Looks like I have to go to Ethiopia."

"When?"

"Tomorrow by noon."

"That's quick."

"That's the job. When duty calls, you drop everything."

"I guess this investigation here is done."

"Guess so. My job is to get rid of bad guys, no questions asked."

"I thought we were getting somewhere on the terror attacks and murders, and the mall attack. But you must do what you gotta do."

"If my stay is short, I'll be back here in no time."

"You better get ready," Reggie said.

"I'm always ready. Every item I own is in the backpack."

Reggie smiled. "Why did I bother asking?"

"I'm efficient."

Reggie and Six walked into the station. Six poured himself a coffee from the self-serve coffee machine and waited in Reggie's office while Reggie went to her superior's office.

IN VIC FALLS, Reggie met with her case officer. He explained the kidnapped or missing daughter of Mr. Osage.

"The billionaire," Reggie said.

"I'm assigning you to a new operation," the man said. "I just got off the phone with the Joburg headquarters. The director wants you on this one, as of yesterday! It's that urgent."

Reggie remained quiet.

"We need answers. These events are getting worse. I need you on this."

"Yes, sir. I'll make my own team."

"Of course. But we are here if you need help," He added. "Didn't want to tell you on the phone, but our intelligence suggests there may be a connection between the kidnapping and what's been going on here."

Reggie remained still. "What about the homicide here?"

"I'm giving it to someone else. Not a priority right now. The director has specifically requested that you be on this one. He said Mr. Osage is important to the Bureau, and we must send the best we have. You are the best we have."

"Care to elaborate? What happened to the girl?"

"That's for you to find out. Every bit of what we know is in this folder. Tomorrow, you fly to Ethiopia to meet with Mr. Osage, then go from there."

"Yes, sir," Reggie said. "To do this I'll need a team I can trust."

"Of course. We will give all the help you need."

"Thank you, sir!"

"And, Reggie, I want this covert. Too many eyes."

"Yes, sir."

Reggie phoned Joyce on her way out, told her that her assignment had changed.

Reggie came back to her office after forty-five minutes carrying a maroon folder. Six sat throwing Reggie's squishy "anxiety ball" against the wall. He swiveled the chair around to face Reggie and stood up.

"Oh no. Sit. I've been sitting for the last forty minutes," Reggie said.

Six returned to the seat and placed his feet on the desk next to the stacks of case folders.

"Mission updates?"

"I've been moved to a new case. Looks like we are both going to Ethiopia. New developments."

Six sat up straight.

Reggie said, "This is weird, but my boss has just assigned me to a new case in Addis Ababa. An 'important client,' he said." She emphasized the quotation marks with fingers on both her hands.

"That's a crazy coincidence."

"It's a possible abduction of a girl. Apparently, the victim is the daughter of an important person to the Agency."

"Who?"

"The report."

Reggie placed the folder on the table.

"Are you thinking what I'm thinking?"

"That it's the same mission as yours?"

"What are the odds?"

"Very low, but not impossible."

"The tickets."

"We are using company wings."

"Sweet."

Reggie opened the folder. "We have a long night ahead."

CHAPTER
TWENTY-ONE

FRESH COFFEE WAS BREWING in the coffeepot. The Vic Falls main conference room was packed with team members called in from different departments including the forensics and chemicals lab teams, logistics, and field agents who had visited the bombing site to collect evidence. Reggie had called an impromptu meeting to discuss the report and the evidence, and strategize.

She and Six stayed late with the experts, going over all the updated files about the Mall of Africa bombing, and studied the files from the other previous attacks. They discussed possible motives and the terrorist fundamentalist groups coming forward claiming responsibility for some of the attacks.

"How many casualties?" Six said.

"Thirty confirmed dead and fifty injured," the logistics officer said.

"Do we know the motivation yet?"

"No one has claimed this attack."

"But why the Mall of Africa?"

"It's a crowded place. Makes a real statement."

"But to what end?" Reggie said.

"Remember what you said," Six said. "I think this attack is a distraction. The kidnapping was the whole point."

"Here is the building's blueprint," said the logistics officer. "The attackers used the basement entrance, away from the cameras. If they really wanted to destroy the place, that would not be the place to bomb. Didn't cause much damage. If the attackers wanted, they could have placed it in a better position."

"So this was a distraction?"

"In my opinion," the officer said.

Six and Reggie exchanged glances.

"None of the main security cameras captured a crime. Nothing unusual, except for this one." The officer played the security camera footage. A blurry image showed the three perpetrators, but their faces were not visible; only their backs in their janitorial overalls. The three men stepped over and around debris and dragged the three girls outside into a black cargo van. Thirty seconds passed, then a man was dragged into the van.

"Who's that guy?" Reggie said, even though she had figured who the man was from the report she had reviewed from her case officer.

"We don't know yet," the logistics officer said. "But by the looks of it, he must to be with the girls."

Reggie nodded. "The bomb was a distraction to capture the girls?"

"Exactly what I'm thinking."

"For ransom?"

"That's a good reason."

"If we can I.D. those girls from the list of

missing people from the mall, we have a chance of tracking the kidnappers and their motivation. Find out if there are any missing teenager names reported."

"Nothing reported yet," Reggie lied.

They reviewed more of the footage from the mall.

"Are these videos legit? Maybe they are deep-fakes," Reggie said, pouring coffee into a Styrofoam cup.

"Yes, all legit. From the only working security camera into the basement garage. We collected all the footage we could salvage. We checked the video camera, and called a couple of van shops in Johannesburg. Found zero. Nothing matches the van. None has a cargo van missing. As you can guess, the company sign, logo, and license plates were fake as well."

"How did security miss this?"

"We questioned all the security and the security chief. Apparently, it's common now to have many repair service people daily, due to frequent load shedding as more appliances are shorting out."

Next, the chemical team that had been hard at work presented their findings on the monitors in front of the room, showing the chemical spectrum analysis.

"Our chemical analysis show aluminum powder traces in the bomb residue collected from the crime scene," said the lead chemist. "This leads us to think the device used was an IED."

"I agree that's a possibility. If it was remotely detonated, it would be impossible to find the perpetrator."

"We are looking at all angles. The lab is analyzing remains from the blast to identify what material was used, and what kind of device was used based on the blast pattern. That may give us a lead."

"Can we figure out where it's from?"

"The serial numbers and markers on the bomb material were filed off or never stamped. Some of the material is not local. Maybe German, French or Chinese. Another possibility is the whole bomb was designed using crude methods, using scrap electronics."

The chemist moved to the next slide showing a reconstruction of the IED.

"Pressure detonation, most likely triggered by a remote control."

"Which means when the bomb went off, the men were already with their targets."

One officer rushed into the room.

"One extremist group in Sudan has claimed the attack!" he said.

Six shook his head. "Those guys only want clout and attention. Any kind of attention is good for them."

"You don't think they did it?" Reggie said.

"No. The Mall of Africa? How would bombing that place be beneficial to them?"

Six listed the different sites and events that had been recorded. "There is a pattern. There must be. We just don't know it yet," he said.

"The earlier attacks were a series of isolated insurrections across Africa, more eastern and central Africa, but we have never had such attacks in southern Africa," Reggie said.

"That's the whole point. They are trying to make it look like just another bombing from extremists," Six said. "Could be an outsider. France losing grip of the Francophone countries, et cetera. Divide and conquer. With no heavy gun factories, where do they get the guns, and funds? Whole goal is to rule by seeding unrest. If you go deep into the mountains of jungles of Sudan to Congo, you find bandits with some crazy firepower. Where the heck do you think they get these?"

"Western companies. I still don't get it. All these years."

"Someone is getting rich from instability. As long as minerals exist in the ground, there'll always going to be civil wars fueled by outsiders."

"And other African countries as well."

"That too. Greed."

"Some reports link it to jihadists or Tigrayan rebels. Other's claim it's from rebels supported by Rwanda."

"Which is which?"

Reggie and Six stayed a few more hours at the office planning for the trip to Addis Ababa the next day.

"I'm still baffled none of the security guards had guns," Six said.

"There's no need. Growing up, I never felt the need to have a gun. And we have never had any civilian mass shootings. Looks like that stuff only happens in the U.S."

"Well, the justification for it is the Second Amendment."

"It's too easy."

"It is too easy!"

"Can't blame the guns, though. They don't shoot people themselves. I think it's mental illness."

TWENTY-TWO

SIX AND REGGIE took a few hours layover in Joburg. Their connection from O.R. Tambo International Airport in the AULEB private jet was scheduled to depart for Addis Ababa at 10:00 a.m. In the meantime, they decided to visit Joyce and the forensics team.

Joyce's team was now stationed on the left wing of the AULEB Headquarters in Joburg, in three full size Biosafety Level 2, 3, and 4 laboratories. Six and Reggie walked along the glossy, tiled hallway. The main morgue had LED lights of different colors, white and yellow.

After checking in on the visitor pads, they put on coveralls, facemasks, booties, gloves, googles, and bouffant caps, and passed through double doors into an air shower, which led into the lab. The lab was slightly darker. Some of the LED lights in the lab were covered with blue cloth. There were four people in the lab. Several bodies lay on exam tables.

Joyce stopped what she was doing on the computer when she saw them. She was wearing sun-glasses.

"Hey, guys," she said. "Glad you made it."

They exchanged pleasantries.

"Hope you don't mind the shades. My eyes have become sensitive to light," Joyce said. "Getting worse with age."

Six and Reggie both shook their heads.

"How're things?" Reggie said.

"We are working hard, as you can see. I'm also still getting used to working in a new space and how the chain of command operates around here. I have some interesting news," Joyce continued. "One of the victims identified at the mall scene turned out to be one of the guards who was supposed to be on duty in that area that day. That's how the terrorists were able to access that restricted basement area of the complex. The terrorists used his I.D. to get in. We estimate he was killed a little over a week before the bomb went off."

"How do you know?"

"Let me show you. They sent the body here for top-level analysis."

Joyce led them to one of the tables. She flung open the white linen that covered the corpse. It reeked. The stench came from embalming fluid and decomposing discolored flesh, in places falling off. The thin layers of skin on his face, sunken eyes, and cheek sockets—barely recognizable. He still had his uniform on.

Joyce continued, "The body was found in a drainage tunnel below the complex. Most of our possible leads are decomposed now. The flesh was almost gone; wild animals and the elements.

Thankfully the concrete slabs protected the basement from the fire and preserved part of the body. Otherwise, they would never have found the body."

Six spoke: "You said the body died a week ago?"

"I'd say it's been almost ten days, to be precise," Joyce said. She used the forceps to pick up a dead fly from the victim's hollow eye sockets. "These are mature flies. It takes ten to fourteen days for maggots to hatch and mature into flies. Thankfully the temperature in those concrete tunnels is cooler, which slowed down decomposition. Otherwise, the whole place would have been stinking and someone would have noticed sooner."

"This means the perpetrators had been there for that long?"

"I suppose."

"So they had all the time they needed to plan the attack. Didn't the management know one of the guards was missing?"

Reggie looked at her phone. "The security manager said in the report that they noticed the guard was missing, but thought he had quit. People quit all the time." She dialed a number and said, "I want to talk to the security manager."

The manager was cooperative, and said it was usual for some of the guards to miss work. He agreed to help as much as he could.

"Ten days is around the same time that you found a body in Vic Falls," Six said.

"What are you thinking?"

"Just piercing a connection together."

"Couldn't be. The murders happened on the

same day," Joyce said. "All between 8:00 and 10:00 p.m."

Six nodded. "Joyce, could you send me this autopsy report when you're done?"

Joyce smiled. "Of course, my prince. Two drinks this time."

They laughed, thanked Joyce, and drove to the airport, where the company jet awaited them.

CHAPTER
TWENTY-THREE

THE JET LANDED at Addis Ababa Bole International Airport at 11:00 a.m. Six and Reggie were led through a separate jet bridge to the lounge where the concierge led them into a grey Land Cruiser 300.

Six received an email from his handler while they were being chauffeured to the restaurant where they were meeting their client. The attachments contained info about their client. The client's name was Chris. His daughter, Colette, had been kidnapped in the mall bombing. An only child. Research showed that Chris was a South African-born American multi-billionaire worth over a hundred billion dollars. His wealth had accrued through biotech and commodity industries. Was still married to his wife of seventeen years, Sheila. Spent his fortune to influence policies across Africa. Outspoken on his Twitter account about his Pan-Africanist views and bashed the West and China. A benefactor to many anti-corruption agencies across Africa and many philanthropic projects across the continent including education and planned parenthood. He was also a board member for many large companies.

The city streets were filled with a tense vibe of excitement and nervousness. Nostalgia hung in the air. There was jubilation as the city decorated for the upcoming Africa Day with banners in multiple languages.

They arrived at the restaurant, a traditional Ethiopian restaurant at the center of downtown Addis Ababa. They made their way through lines of patrons, into the dimly lit dining room, with a backdrop of Arabic music playing. The restaurant was packed at this hour.

The server called them by name. "Welcome, Mr. George and Ms. Reggie. This way."

She led them to a private booth away from other patrons. They marveled at the colorful mosaic chandeliers above each table and several murals on the walls. The aromas of fresh coffee and spices wafted throughout the restaurant. The server seated them. Six changed his seat so he sat facing the entrance.

Chris arrived five minutes later from the restroom.

"Ah, Detective Kona and Agent Six. What a pleasure."

They shook hands. Chris' eyes were puffed and red from lack of sleep and his voice was hoarse.

"I've heard a lot about you two."

"Thank you, Mr. Osage," Reggie and Six replied in unison.

"Please call me Chris."

They nodded.

"Your reputation precedes you. Reggie, your boss recommended you two after what you did in

Victoria Falls with the corrupt minister. You are the only two people I can trust right now. I don't even trust my colleagues in the council. A friend of mine, Mr. Biles, recommended you during one of my golf matches a few months back. He said you saved his children. You know word travels fast, especially for people with our privilege, always looking over our shoulders for a day like this, even though you hope it never comes to that. But I need your help. I have already wired the payments to your accounts."

Chris recounted the kidnapping and the mysterious phone call.

"My daughter has been abducted," Chris said. "I met with you here alone because I don't believe my wife can bear any more pain."

His countenance was stoic, revealing no emotion. But one could feel the pain in the man's voice and manner.

"You surprise me, Mr. Osage," Six said. "You seem not in the least emotional about your daughter's abduction."

"Believe me, I cried enough the last two days. I'm a man of action. Whining and wailing won't save my daughter."

"You have enemies from across the aisle who hate that you support Pan-Africanist ideologies," Reggie said. "How much money are they demanding?"

"No money. They want a document. It will be here tonight. My men are ready, but I need your help making sure it gets here safely from the airport, via Mr. Fernando Mussa, my fellow Pan-Africanist."

"You know Mussa?" Reggie said.

"Yes. How did you think he had access to security and private jets? That was the only way he survived that long with all the enemies he has."

"What's this document?"

"It'll be easier to explain if you can see it."

"When will his plane arrive?"

Chris looked at his Rolex Submariner. "At seven this evening."

"We have some time."

"Please be available just in case, at a distance. I don't know whom to trust among my people, so I have to trust you two."

"Why did you want to meet in Addis Ababa?"

"I decided to leave Joburg for a few days to be here, where I am not so recognizable. I think someone close to me might have given them information about my meeting. At first I was supposed to meet Mussa in Tangier."

"Shouldn't we be focused on finding your daughter?" Reggie said.

"I think it's all connected. Help me get Mussa here and we can go from there. If we can find the people who are after the document, that may lead us to my daughter."

Then Chris explained the connections between the six bombings and assassinations. He said, "These were coordinated attacks. We suspected someone was leaking information out. And the hotel murder was bait. We had used a double, and they fell for it. Now we know for sure someone is after the document. It's safely stashed in a doomsday bunker, strong enough to survive a nuclear blast or an asteroid attack. The whole earth can be wiped out and this structure would still be standing and everything in it."

"That was clever," Reggie said.

"Who was the double?"

"A man with a few weeks to live from pancreatic cancer. His family received a small fortune for his service to the continent's cause. Professional makeup can do wonders."

"Chris, who else knew your daughter would be at the mall?"

"Me, my wife, the bodyguards, and the housekeeper. And her friends' parents."

"Could it be the bodyguard?" Six said.

"No. He was like a big brother to Colette. Been here since she was born. He is dead now. Bullet to the head."

"I see."

"Why would someone want to kidnap your daughter?"

"As a person of wealth, I have a lot of enemies. But I don't know who would do such a thing."

"Think harder. Who else might be involved?"

"Could be some company wanting to get the railway contract," Chris said. "My people have investigated that route. We don't see a reason yet."

"About the call from the kidnappers, how much time do we have?" Reggie said.

"They haven't said, yet. They said I should wait for coordinates for the drop zone."

"I'd say we have seventy-two hours to get to the bottom of this," Six said. "What else do you know?"

Chris spoke: "Colette attempted an SOS call in a village just north of Maputo. My guys searched the whole area. Questioned everyone. But it was a dead end. All they could find were the phones and watches from the kids. No one in the area had seen them. Dead end. Remember these are parts of Mozambique you can go for kilometers and kilometers without seeing a single soul."

"Let's get Mussa here safely. Then we go from there," Reggie said.

"I'll have my guys send you everything you need," Chris said.

The server brought the meal: injera rolls, chicken, chickpeas, kale, red lentils, and a salad in vinaigrette dressing. While they were eating, a young woman came to the table and said to Chris, "Boss, it is all good to go. I will see you in a few days."

Six and Reggie looked up at her. Six was shocked.

"Ophélie!"

Reggie looked at Six, then at the woman, confused.

"James George! Or should I call you Six?"

"What are you doing here?"

"Working. You?"

Six looked at Chris. "Don't tell me she works for you?"

"I'm guessing you already met," Chris said.

"We met, all right," Six said.

"We are both liars, aren't we?" Ophélie said.

"Should have known," Six said. "Trouble seems to follow me around."

"Story of my life!" Ophélie said. "How was the rest of your trip in Lyon?"

Reggie looked at Six wide-eyed.

"Perhaps," she said, "you would like to introduce me to Ophélie?"

"Don't worry. She meant no harm," Chris hastily said. "Ophélie is a former French intelligence operative. She works for me now. She was just checking Six after reports he might be selling intelligence to other governments, using the files you obtained from the minister before his untimely death."

"You know her?" Reggie said to Six. "She called you James George."

"We've met once," Six said.

"Where?"

Six ignored Reggie's question, and said, "Mr. Osage, you sent her after me?"

"No. Rather, we convinced her to tell us your whereabouts. That's how we knew you were in Lyon."

"If you harmed her, I will break your leg!"

"Calm down. She's fine. No force was used. She is a fine asset for us."

"I'd really like to hear more about this," Reggie said.

"We are on the same side," said Chris. "Who do you think sponsored the AULEB or CID?"

"Let me guess. You did?"

"Correct, Detective Kona. My shell company sponsored the AU Intelligence and Law Enforcement Bureau, your employer. I and a civilian with the means to effect change were the benefactors. And, Detective Kona, your boss knows this."

Reggie was stunned.

Chris said, "Who did you think was the rainmaker for all the resources you use, and who vouched for you for that promotion?"

"From what you said, I'm guessing it was you," Reggie said.

"Yes. Wanted to change the motherland for the better."

Six said to Reggie, "You and I and Ophélie are on the same team."

"I sent her to find you," Chris said to Six. "That's what she does. And she is good at it."

"I will go to Morocco now and see what I can find. I know some people," Ophélie said.

"Alone?" Six said.

"Don't worry. I'm good at getting information."

"She is good," Chris said. "She's the one who told us about the possible attack in Tangier before it happened. That was fortunate, because we were planning a meeting there."

"Okay," Reggie said, taking her napkin out of her lap and placing it on the table "Mr. Osage, we will catch up with you after tonight. Latest by early morning."

"Please stay seated. There is yet time," said Chris. "I haven't said all I need to say to you."

Ophélie nodded at her boss and left.

TWENTY-FOUR

CHRIS SMILED. "Mussa will be bringing the document in a briefcase like this one," he said, unlocking an obviously expensive model of briefcase. Taking out a folder, he opened it and read, "Draye Sixpence. Left tackle on the Southwestern Community College football team. Six years in the U.S. Marines. Four tours in the Middle East. Parents killed when—"

Six stood up, practically knocking over his seat; Chris was saying too much. Chris's bodyguards stepped up.

"Should I go on?" Chris said.

"Do not mention my parents. How do you know all that?"

"When you get to my level of prominence," said Chris, "you have to have those resources. As a sponsor of AU Intelligence, I can dig up info about anyone. I've the resources to get any information I want, from some of the toughest intelligence agencies, given some time. I just don't have time on this one."

"But you were not so thorough about checking

out possible hazards where your daughter was going?"

Chris was quiet for a moment and then said, "Let me ask you this, Mr. Sixpence. Have you wondered why NEPHRON picked you up?"

Six remained silent.

"You think it was maybe serendipity?" said Chris.

"If you know things I don't, you had better tell me now."

"Your father worked for us," Chris said. "That accident was no accident. He was a target. Ever wonder why he never visited friends or his family often?"

"And my mother?"

"Collateral damage. Wrong place, wrong time."

"Did you catch who killed them?"

"No, but we suspected someone."

"Who?"

"The same people who are after our leaders now."

"What was my father working on that he was killed?"

"A document."

"Is this the same document we were talking about? What's with this document?"

"Yes. This document will potentially bring Africa together."

Six paused and thought about what Chris had said. But again, he barely remembered his father. He was rarely at home. Six knew only that his father had been his hero. Six was nine years old when his parents died in a car accident. It felt like ages ago now.

"What's in it for you?" Reggie said, looking at Chris. "This whole bringing Africa together?"

"Just satisfaction of doing what's right. A legacy."

"No one does anything without some type of compensation."

"That is true. In my view, I'm gaining peace of mind. Look, I've all the wealth I need. I can buy multiple countries. After that, then what?"

"There has to be more?" Six said.

"Peace. The end of world poverty. I'm sick of the same story."

Six and Reggie remained quiet.

"I've all I could ever want. See, being a billionaire affords you anything. I literally mean anything. I could be everywhere, with anyone, doing anything I want with just a single phone call. But that's all vanity to me. I'd rather buy time, resources, and change international policies."

"You expect us to believe that you're doing this out of your own benevolence."

"That's what I said, isn't it?"

The agents kept their faces neutral.

"Anyway. Doesn't matter what I say. What defines me is what I do. My actions speak louder than all the talking and promises I could ever make. I always prided myself on actually meeting goals other people only talk about. I have conquered business. But this excites me more. Imagine the benefits for future generations. They might never know I orchestrated this. But that's okay. I know the ancestors are smiling upon me.

"I can't stop now. And I will keep doing this even if it affects my family—my daughter. Colette would be disappointed if I stop now. It's my purpose."

"Do you plan to run for office?" Six said.

"No."

"Then why are you doing all this?"

"My legacy. For my daughter and future generations. None of us live forever. We can only do that through our children and what we create. I want to leave this world better than I've found it. God has blessed me so much."

"How do you know the AULEB director?" Reggie said.

"Gerald and I go way back. We met when he was only a detective."

"That makes sense."

"I'm an advocate for change that I'd like to see. Unity across the continent. A goal our forefathers died for. And someone hates me for having the resources to make it happen. And has taken my daughter. They might be the same people."

Six and Reggie left the restaurant and freshened up at the hotel before heading to the airport to receive the escort the delegate.

During the drive, they had learned the delegate was Fernando Mussa, the former president of Tanzania. He was also the Chairman of the African Union Assembly, a group of heads of state that met once a year to discuss the future of the continent. Mussa was a respected patriot, and chairman of the African States Coalition, chief organization of the Pan-Africanist Movement. As a staunch Pan-Africanist he was vocal about the West's involvement in Africa, particularly France's stronghold in the Sahel and central Africa. He pushed for limited terms in office in a continent filled with leaders who clung to power till they died. Known for always wearing a Pan-Africanist traditional shirt with faces of the prominent Pan-Africanism movement forefathers plastered all over it. As a leader he was notorious for thumbing down on corruption, kickbacks, and lobbying. Most major firms hated Mussa's approach on taxes, as he aimed to increase taxes on the rich, and he had held big companies, politicians, policy makers, and two former presidents accountable, tracking all their offshore financial trails when he was the director of the anti-corruption agency. He was the force that gathered the committee comprised of delegates from across the continent, elected to sign the document.

TWENTY-FIVE

THE HIT SQUAD waited for the convoy at the intersection a few kilometers from the airport. They had specific instructions: Secure Mussa and the document and kill everyone else. The squad timed the collision as the former president's motorcade was halfway through the crossroads. Chaos! Shooting!

Three blocks away, Six and Reggie had at that moment pulled the Land Cruiser up to an intersection when they heard a loud bang followed by semiautomatic gunshots and sirens. They had decided not to drive nearer to the airport but station themselves at that intersection as an added precaution for when the delegate arrived. Reggie watched the police officer who was directing the congested traffic in the middle of the road with his hands and a whistle. Sirens and gunfire. Seconds later, a ball of fire erupted, sending smoke plumes over the skyline.

"It's going down!" Reggie said.

"That's three blocks from here."

"Go, go!"

Six honked, but the traffic didn't move. Six swerved the cruiser onto the gravel embankment, knocking off stones, containers, and fruit stands operated by roadside vendors, and cut through the grass. He kept honking, smashing through makeshift shacks down the alley. They emerged on the other side where they could see the scene from a few yards away. The whole place was a battle zone. Smoke, bullets raining, screams, yelling in multiple languages.

Cars had piled on each other blocking the intersection; drivers and pedestrians were running in all directions. Several bodies lay motionless on the pavement.

A stray bullet smashed the side window of the Land Cruiser. "Crap!" Reggie said, and ducked, and pulled out her handgun.

The car swerved from side to side, then Six steadied it. Bullets kept coming, embedding in the car's chassis.

"Take the wheel," Six said, steadying the cruiser next to buildings shielding it from open fire. "I will deal with these guys."

Reggie squeezed her way into the driver's seat and slowed down in the face of oncoming gunfire. Six picked up and cocked the semiautomatic rifle on the back seat. He aimed it through the smashed window and started shooting, knocking the assassins off one by one with precision.

"We need to get to the dignitary!"

Reggie revved the car into the cloud of smoke. They both jumped out of the Land Cruiser and crouched behind it, hearing sounds, screams, and the thud of bodies falling everywhere. Bodies of the delegate's security detail.

"He is somewhere."

In time the shooting subsided. More and more police cars and ambulances arrived at the scene, sirens blaring. They all helped the injured and drove them off to the hospital. Paramedics too rushed people to the hospital.

Reggie and Six separated. Six took a gas mask from a dead body on the ground. Someone had prepared very well for this scene. They both searched in the smoke for the dignitary's vehicle with the briefcase that Chris had described.

Six found Mussa, groaning, in a cruiser flipped upside down, its fuel leaking. Six debated whether to leave him, but decided to take him because the car might catch fire. With effort, Six pulled Mussa out of the flipped car and carried him towards an ambulance. Behind him, Mussa's car suddenly exploded, and the force thrust them both into the pavement. For an instant, fire seemed to engulf them.

First responders ran up and strapped Mussa to a trauma board and loaded him onto a cot. Two paramedics rushed in to help them load Mussa into an ambulance.

Six declined treatment and decided to accompany Mussa to the hospital. The ambulance backed out immediately from the cloud of smoke, and its siren sounded. There were three other ambulances in front of them. Six sat holding Mussa's hand.

Six phoned Reggie. "I found him. Heading east to the hospital."

"Okay. I'm right behind you."

Six turned to Mussa.

The two EMTs in the ambulance wore protective medical gear. After strapping Mussa to the stretcher, one of them took a vial and a syringe from the medication bag and extended the delegate's arm to inject the liquid.

"What is that?" Six said, under his heavy mask.

"Epinephrine."

"Shouldn't you wait for the ICU doctor to do that?"

"Half of his body is fried. Second- and third-degree burns. If we do not do it now, we will lose him. Likely to have respiratory failure."

The man emptied the vial contents into the syringe and steadied the needle trying to find a vein on the burned arm of the man strapped to the cot. The van ran over a pothole and the empty vial rolled towards Six. He picked it up and read the label.

"Man, this is not adrenaline! What—?"

A blow from the fire extinguisher knocked Six out before he could finish. He flew into the metal wall of the ambulance and groaned.

The EMT wielding the fire extinguisher lunged towards Six, ready to smash his brains out. Then the ambulance suddenly braked, sending both men plummeting toward the front of the van. Seconds later the back doors swung open as the ambulance lurched forward, sending Six and the other man sliding backwards. Six clung to the railing on the swinging back door, while his assailant wasn't as fortunate. He missed the door and flew off onto the tarmac. His head cracked and his body rolled several feet to the roadside. Dead. The other EMT reached for a gun from beneath his scrubs, but Six was swinging slightly on the gaping ambulance door, and when the EMT fired twice, the bullets missed Six, but narrowly. The ambulance ran over another pothole. The EMT stumbled, losing the gun. The ambulance door winged close enough for Six to jump back into the van. Six leaped at the EMT. As a unit they crashed against the interior wall. The gun misfired, hitting the driver in the arm. The driver yelped. The ambulance swayed from side to side, plowing into the sides of an embankment. Six and his assailant rolled on the van floor, wrestling each other for the gun. Six kicked the EMT's head with his heel then crawled towards the gun while the EMT clung to Six's leg—the only leverage he had to keep from flying out of the van. Six stretched, just reaching the gun with a fingertip. He aimed and fired four times into the man's head mask. Brain tissue decorated the van ceiling. The second EMT's body flew out the gaping back door of the ambulance and crashed into the pavement.

By now they were being followed.

Six jumped out from the box and darted to the front. He yanked open the passenger door and pointed his gun at the driver, who was clutching his bicep, trying to block the blood flowing from his arm. The driver trembled.

Six climbed in and pressed the gun on the man's left ribs.

"Please, don't kill me! I'm just a driver."

"Count this your lucky day," Six barked. "Keep driving!"

The driver was reduced to steering with one hand. Six searched him, found a phone, and threw it out of the window.

Six eyed the wound. "It's a flesh wound. You will be fine. Can you drive?"

The man nodded.

"I need you to get to a hospital. Take a left. Fast! Fast!"

The ambulance veered into the gravel through a high-density residential area of shacks, with people selling items along the roads. Six looked in the rear-view mirror. In the car following the ambulance a man wearing glasses was leveling a rifle, ready to shoot. Then the car disappeared.

"We lost them," the driver said.

"Good. Take a left."

The driver obliged.

"Reggie," Six said into his phone, "I have the target. In the ambulance. Going out. Let's go."

"I'm right behind."

In the rear-view mirror, Reggie's battered Land Cruiser came into view.

They drove for several blocks with no one behind them.

"We lost the briefcase!" Reggie said.

"Screw the briefcase. I need answers! We are losing him fast!" Six told Reggie. "Call Chris! Get the paramedics ready!"

Six ordered the driver to stop beneath an over-pass. Reggie arrived shortly. She and Six transferred Mussa and the ambulance driver into the back of the Land Cruiser, then set the ambulance on fire. Six jumped into the driver's seat and slammed the car into drive. They screeched back onto the main road.

"Mr. Mussa, you're safe now," Reggie said.

"Who're you?" The man said as he faded into and out of consciousness. "Who—who are you?"

Reggie checked his pulse.

"Faster," she told Six. "We are losing him!"

CHAPTER
TWENTY-SIX

SIX TOOK A LEFT, then a right two blocks down, then circled through the other side of town. Satisfied they were not being tailed, he headed towards Chris's Addis Ababa residence.

At the estate, Mussa was carried to the infirmary while a paramedic bound the ambulance driver's arm. Then the driver was handcuffed and dragged to another cottage. An aide led Six and Reggie to the backyard. The grounds were teeming with aides and security guards.

They found Chris, his wife, and a dog sitting on a wooden swing behind the courtyard overlooking the infinity pool. The swing creaked slightly.

"Sir, Detective Kona and Mr. Six are here."

They waited while Chris remained silent and gazing into the distance.

"Sir—"

"Ah, Detective Thandie Kona, and Agent Six!" Chris said. He dismissed the aide. "Thank you, Robert. You may leave us. Welcome to my home, Agent Six and Detective Kona. This is my wife, Sheila, and our dog, M.J.!"

Both Reggie and Six shook Sheila's hand. "Nice to meet you, Mrs. Osage."

"Please call me Sheila. I insist."

Reggie and Six nodded.

Chris spoke. "Tell me, what do you see when you look in the horizon?"

"That the sun has set?" Reggie said.

"Beautiful, isn't it? To me it's more than that. The water is life itself. The waves, how they whisper, beating the edges back and forth and never giving up."

Six and Reggie remained quiet.

"That's life, isn't it?" Chris looked up at the pair, not seeing that they were disheveled and sweaty or noticing they smelled of smoke. He was lost in his own thoughts.

"After I had spinal surgery," Chris said "I almost died. The pool was the only sanctuary. A place I could find therapy. I would sit on my porch for hours and hours, and the pain seemed to dissipate. That's why I like this place. It's therapy."

Six said, "Chris, why did they want Mussa dead? If we had not been there in time, he would be dead. They tried twice. Their firepower was coordinated and organized, which leads me to believe these are not amateurs."

Chris looked at Sheila. "This is the second attempted assassination of a high-profile AU delegate. The last one was in Tangier two days ago."

"Oh, dear God," said Sheila.

"As I said earlier," Chris said. "Our intelligence report had warned that there would be an attack, so the guy in Tangier was a decoy. Confirming the reports. I can't trust anyone here except you two."

"Why Mussa?"

"He is the only signature not yet on the document."

"He's in a bad way. Is he safe here?"

"This is the safest place right now," Chris said. "He or you can have anything you need brought to you here in addition to what I already have."

LATER, in private, Chris, with his wife still clinging to him, described to them the structure of the compound, now guarded 24/7 with armed private sentries. The place had an underground doomsday bunker with a situation room comprised of the latest technology, and an artillery room. The food vault had supplies enough to last for two years and they were continuously being recycled as they neared their expiration dates. There were cupboards full of pouches of Meals-Ready-to-Eat. Solar power and lithium power packs meant the estate could operate completely off-grid.

Reggie said, "Chris, what are you not telling us? If you want your daughter, we need to know the truth, and in detail."

Chris looked at Six, then at his wife, then out through a window. Chris apologized to Six and Reggie.

"I should have told you this earlier. My motto is duty over self," Chris said. "But I failed my family. I'm starting to question if all of what I'm doing is worth risking my family's lives."

"About the document," Reggie said. "Mussa's briefcase was destroyed."

"That's fine. There was nothing in it. Hopefully

whoever is after the document will believe it was destroyed. I wanted the man, not the document. And now I know there is someone on my team giving out information. Their belief that Mussa had possession of that document was the only thing that kept Mussa alive. If they got the document, they would just kill him."

"Where is this document if it's not with him?"

"It is called Document Number One. At the first African Union meeting in Ghana in 1960, a document was drafted by Pan-Africanist leaders for each country's representatives to sign. The goal was to create a unified Africa. They called it the Declaration of United African States, DUAS. A unified Africa as one country, under one flag, emulating the United States' founding principles. Among all the representatives, some voted against it, evidently with foreign influence."

"Never heard of it."

"The leaders believed it was the most important document in African history, the African analogue to the Magna Carta or the U.S. Declaration of Independence. Their goal was to build a constitutional libertarian nation and lessen the power of politicians. Yes, everyone will say I am doing this to fatten my pockets at the expense of billions of people. But someone has to do it."

"Where is this document?"

"In a safe place."

"How did you come to possess this document?"

"My grandfather bought it. Authenticated. I will have it brought to us and show you."

CHAPTER
TWENTY-SEVEN

IN A FEW MINUTES an armed guard brought a box and unlocked it for Chris. Inside was the Declaration, dated April 25, 1960, signed by heads of all its African member states except one. Six and Reggie studied the yellow, aged document in awe.

"I want you to find who ordered the killing of my man in Tangier," Chris said to Six and Reggie. "If they get a hold of the document, then the African Union dream is gone."

Six and Reggie glanced at each other.

"This document is our only hope for finding my daughter," Chris said.

"Why do you move the physical copy? Wouldn't it be easier to move digital copies?" Six said.

"Cyber warfare. It's a secret document. Digital copies will be released only when all the signatures are on it. On Africa Day," Chris said. "This original carries more than half a century of dreams."

Chris locked the box and tucked it beneath his arm.

"I would appreciate it," said Reggie, "if you stayed out of the way and let us do our job."

"Of course, I'll stay out of your way. My wife needs me during this time."

"Thank you."

"I received a message from Ophélie that she might have some leads in Morocco."

"Okay," said Chris. "Then you take my jet there. To get started you will need better wheels. I will have delivered at the airstrip in Morocco a new Land Cruiser. You have me on speed dial if you have any needs whatsoever."

Six and Reggie excused themselves and took showers in two of the thirteen bathrooms on the estate to wash off the blood, smoke, and dirt. Then the house nurse tended to their minor bruises. After cleaning up, Tali took them to the artillery room where they refreshed their firearms and picked up new ones of their choice.

CHAPTER
TWENTY-EIGHT

MUBARAK'S MEN had reached the Republic of the Congo and Mubarak's compound at night. Upon arrival, the three teenage girls were unbound, and given buckets to bathe with, then thrown into a cell in the cellblock behind the garage. Each received a thin cotton cloth for a blanket. It was dark and damp, really a dungeon. They were next to a dormitory where several child laborers stayed, both boys and girls. Most were malnourished.

Colette had woken up the next morning with muddy boots shoving her. A guard dragged her from the cell through a courtyard into a side door of what looked like the main house. They turned left into a passageway to the dining room. The guard introduced Colette to his boss. Mubarak sat in a gold-plated reclining chair at the head of the long banquet table with nineteen empty chairs around it. Behind his chair was a large golden eagle sculpture with wide open wings and talons.

Ugly, Colette thought, the moment she saw Mubarak. He had a deep slash mark, a scar, on his face from the left of his forehead, past his eye and nose, and ending right below the chin. Cigar in hand, he wore a purple and gold robe of old Victorian design, embroidered Western style with castle pillars topped with blue spires. He sat alone, an array of pastries and fruit in front of him. His butler stood to the side.

Mubarak smiled, exposing stained yellow teeth. "Sit!" he said.

The guard forced Colette into a chair at the end of the long refectory table.

Mubarak took a long puff of the cigar and let out a white stream of smoke. He smiled again and said, "You're in a rarefied space, young lady. Do you know who has dined in this hall, sat in these chairs?" He spread his hands to emphasize his point and paused, then said, "Princes, heads of states, presidents, have all been here, and of course poor souls like yourself who find themselves in here by fate."

Colette remained quiet.

"At this massive dining table have sat secret corporate representatives and politicians from the West, Middle East, and China."

Mubarak beckoned the butler to bring Colette some food. The butler brought a plateful of croissants and grapes, bowed, and left the table to stand in his spot.

"Eat!"

Colette refused to eat. Mubarak raised his voice and said, "Young lady, in our culture it's disrespectful to refuse food as a guest when it's offered to you. Do you know how many people in this country don't have anything to eat?"

Colette tried to ignore him.

Mubarak said, "Do you know why you are here?"

Colette looked at him, then the food. She did not answer.

"Your father has something that I want. And he is going to give me that thing, for me alone." He took a bite of a pastry, then said, "Now do you think your father loves you enough to let his daughter suffer for a document?"

Mubarak pointed at Colette his silver table knife.

"If your father does not give me what I want, do you know what will happen to you?"

Colette remained quiet.

"Young lady, you will answer when I ask you a question."

The guard next to Colette shoved a gun into her ribs.

"My dad will find you and kill you!" she finally said.

"Oh, will he?" Mubarak said. He burst into laughter.

"He will kill you!"

Mubarak stood up and approached Colette. He gripped her jaw and strained her neck upwards. "No one answers like that to me in my castle. I'm the king!" He shoved her back into the armchair and plopped back into his own chair. Colette wiped flecks of Mubarak's saliva from her face with the back of her hand.

"Now listen. Your father has an item that I want. And I will make him get it to me. If he doesn't, whatever happens to you is on his hands. He will come crawling to me after that. And your life will be hell. I'm sure you've seen the living conditions of your neighbors here."

Mubarak motioned with his hand for the guard to remove Colette from his presence.

As soon as Colette left, he ordered his other guards out of the dining room. Then Mubarak made a phone call.

"It's done," Mubarak said. "We have the girl, and we expect the document within a few days."

"Great job," the woman from the other side said. "I knew you were the man for the job."

Mubarak beamed. The phone call ended. He poured himself a glass of whiskey and extended the reclining sofa, then turned the TV and watched cartoons. Life was good, and so easy.

TWENTY-NINE

EARLIER THAT DAY, Ophélie met with her informant in Tangier. The contact's name was Clément, a former member of the French foreign agency Ophélie had once worked for. Although not in the same department, they had both done basic training together before being assigned to different operations in Africa: she as part of the intelligence, and he as a ground officer of the foreign brigade.

The two met at sundown outside the Mendoubia Gardens. The area was getting crowded. They sat on two benches opposite each other. Ophélie placed her handbag on her knees and rested her hands on it. She observed Clément's uneasiness. She had a gun if he attempted anything stupid. Ophélie noticed Clément's dramatic weight loss. She remembered him being fit. But now he was frail, even wearing a heavy coat in the warm weather.

Clément looked at Ophélie, then away, aware of the way she had looked at him.

Ophélie spoke, "Thank you for meeting with me."

"What did you want to know? Be quick, I don't trust anyone here."

"Where is he?"

"I don't know. Word around says he might be here in town."

"How do you know that?"

"Guys in the streets. When we are dealing, they talk. Brought in more product."

"Have you seen him?"

"Me? No. I don't want to see no devil. I hope I never see that man again." Clément looked around. "I heard it's only me and him left from our brigade. Don't know if it's true."

"You said you knew where the girl is?"

"I think so," he said. "I distributed the product a couple months back for him. Back then, he was operating in Mombasa. I saw him with a little girl that looked like him. Not sure if it's—what was her name?"

"Katy," Ophélie prompted him.

"Not sure if it's Katy, but he treated her differently."

Ophélie took a photo from her purse and showed it to him. "Is this the girl?"

Clément studied the image in the fading daylight. "Yes, that's her. I remember."

"How do I get to her?"

"I know the area and the address. Do you have a pen and paper? Yeah, you know I'm a junkie now, but my mind is still sharp as a whistle. I remember everything. Even the bad things we did. I wish I could forget."

Ophélie handed him a notepad and a pen from her handbag. Clément wrote the address and returned the note.

"Thank you."

"You didn't hear it from me. Good luck finding the little girl. Who is this girl?"

"A missing person," Ophélie said. "What were you doing in Mombasa?"

"Business. Moving product for the boss onto the ships to Europe, Asia and some to the Americas.

"After the agency, I was lost. No family. No job. He gave me a job. The money was good. My plan was to get in, make enough money, and quit. But before long, I was in too deep to get out. Those people can't just let you leave the ring. Only way out is death. I was reckless and messed up my health."

"How did you get out?"

"I ran away. Got on a plane as usual, transporting some swallowed Triple Z to France. Which I would vomit in France and sell. Had made the same trip many times, but I wanted out. Left and never went back. I just hope they don't find me. I'm dead anyway."

"You have been on the run this whole time?"

"Yes," he said. "Until you contacted me. If you can find me, I know they can, too. If I were you, I'd be very careful."

"I can take care of myself." Ophélie felt the weight of the revolver in her handbag.

Clément stood up and left. Two minutes later, Ophélie stood up and walked downhill in the other direction. She booked a ticket to Mombasa on her phone and headed to the airport. She texted Reggie and Six.

CHAPTER THIRTY

AT THE OSAGE ESTATE, Chris's maids fit Six and Reggie with clean clothes while a guard went to their hotel rooms to pack their bags and bring them to the airstrip.

When they came downstairs Chris said, "The nurse has called. Mr. Mussa is awake. Stabilized."

Six, Reggie, and Chris, the locked box beneath his arm, rushed to the infirmary where Mussa was receiving treatment.

Reggie had noticed Six squeezing his shoulder, scraped from pulling Mussa from his crushed and leaking vehicle.

"You should have the nurse check that out," Reggie said.

"I'll be fine," Six said.

Mussa was hooked up to drips of saline and other drugs. He had third-degree burns on his legs and second-degree burns on his arms and parts of his face, all bandaged. He spoke in a feeble yet powerful voice.

"I understand I must thank you for saving me."

"We were there just in time, sir," Reggie said.

"What happened?"

"You were in a hit. We believe someone wanted you dead."

There was concern in Mussa's eyes. He touched his forehead with the bandaged hand.

Reggie spoke. "The ambulance was burned to the ground so that law enforcement couldn't identify the remains, now ash and soot. News and the media broadcast your assassination. You had survived several attempts before. The rest of the world thinks you are dead."

Mussa nodded, then closed his weary eyes for a long moment.

"Do we know who is behind this attack?" Mussa finally said.

"Our own African counterintelligence suggests France maybe involved," Reggie said. "But they have denied any involvement in the attacks."

"Of course they would deny," Mussa said. "It's geopolitics. Many people would want me dead based on my political stance. But the document is safe?"

"Yes. Ready to sign when you are ready."

"I'll do it right now."

Chris opened the lockbox and lifted out the document, and Mussa signed his name, the final necessary signature, and tears began running down his burned face. The nurse quickly sponged them away.

Six looked at the former president. "Why did you wait so long to sign the document?"

"Political blackmail. They have a record of what I once did, and it would have come out if I voted for the bill."

"You do someone's bidding against your morals?"

"I lost my morals the second I decided to become a politician."

"Who is 'they' that have this record?"

"Do this job long enough, and greed, power, and corruption will overcome your decency."

"Come clean," said Six. "This has to end now."

"This will destroy my wife, my kids and all I've worked for. They have film of me at—"

"They will kill you anyway. Better do what's right. Nothing to lose. Either way, you're dead," Six said.

"I know that now. God is with me. The ancestors are with me," Mussa said, then groaned, and asked that the nurses lower the head of his hospital bed. "I'll see this through. I have survived so many times. I don't have it in me to die. I have been saved for a purpose."

"Who stands to benefit from your death? Corporations? The CIA?"

"Who knows? Any of them could be. This whole operation is complex with layers I don't even want to fathom."

"We will undo it layer by layer."

"Story is always the same. Like what Kissinger said, 'There are no permanent friends.' One day you are a friend of the West, the next you're vilified as the worst enemy."

"Well, you are a friend as long as you play along to their prerequisites."

"True."

Chris took the signed document and returned it to its case.

"Our goal is to ratify the declaration on Africa

Day, May 25," Chris said. "Chairman Mussa, you must lead the union until we can have the first fair elections."

Mussa seemed to have drifted off into sleep.

"He is the only one I think really has a passion for our people," said Chris. "Everyone else is just hungry for power. I know most leaders across the continent respect him."

"Let's keep it that way until after the voting when the declaration passes," Reggie said.

"Let's find out from the prisoner why they wanted Mussa dead. We might find where Colette is," said Six.

They left the infirmary for the cottage where the ambulance driver was being held.

CHAPTER
THIRTY-ONE

NEXT DOOR, Tali and his crew had been interrogating the driver from the ambulance for more than an hour.

Tali entered the room where Chris, Six and Reggie were. His sleeves were rolled up, his hands and white dress shirt bloody and wet. He used a handkerchief to wipe blood off his hands and knuckles. When the ambulance driver had been brought in, Tali and crew did the torturing. The driver's bullet-grazed arm was treated, and then the interrogation started.

"Boss, we tried everything," Tali told them. "The guy did not budge. Electricity, cutting the skin, but he insists he doesn't know about the mall bombing or abduction of a girl."

Chris nodded. "What does he say about the attempted assassination this evening?"

"Maintains he was paid to drive cargo. Didn't know there was going to be people shooting and dying. Says he doesn't know who hired him. An online message, and a link with one-quarter of the payment."

"This trail leads to somewhere."

"A dead end. The person who did the hiring used numbers from a prepaid voucher."

"You believe him?"

"People usually break with the methods we use. We can go further, sir, if you wish it so. Waterboarding, pulling nails."

Chris deliberated the point. "That's enough for today," Chris said.

"Okay, boss. I'll tell my guys to return him to his holding room."

"Where is he now?"

"Recovering. He tried to kill himself. Remember, he lost a lot of blood from the earlier bullet hole. He passed out after I smashed his face into the table, and he started having convulsions and went into shock. We were able to resuscitate him."

"Let's keep him alive. He may be our only hope of finding Colette."

"He did say, 'We are everywhere. Every move you make, we are a step ahead,' and that the attack in Tangier will give us answers of more to come. He said, 'If you kill me, you will never find those girls. I'm not afraid of death'."

Six said, "I'm not buying his bluff. Give it a day or so. He will break."

Chris's cellphone buzzed. He answered.

"Osage, you think you are clever, huh?" It was a coarse voice, electronically enhanced.

Chris looked at Reggie, Six and Tali. Tali nodded. The phone was tapped and the conversation was being recorded.

The voice said, "Listen to me very carefully. Here's the plan. You have until May 24 to bring that document to me. If you do anything stupid between now and then, your daughter dies. By the way, she believes in you. She believes you'll come and save her and kill me." The voice laughed.

"That's in a few days. Where?"

"I know you have one of my men," the voice said. "Give him the document, leave him un-harmed, then I will give back your daughter. We will do an exchange at the square in front of the AU Headquarters at 9:00 p.m. on Africa Day. I will be watching."

"How do I know you'll keep your word?"

"You don't. But you look to me like a man who will do anything to save his daughter. Aren't you, Osage?"

Chris remained quiet.

"Remember, by May 24!"

The call ended.

CHAPTER
THIRTY-TWO

THE LOCALS CALLED it *Ndako monene*. *Ndako monene* was Mubarak's residence. In the local Lingala language this meant *The Mansion*. Mubarak's compound was perched in a forest in the middle of nowhere, on two thousand hectares of land he owned. Most of the land was acquired from villagers violently displaced. For the next ten to twenty miles every direction there were no inhabitants, only thick hardwood forests and mines.

Colette had taken inventory of what she had seen outside. To escape, there were several hurdles. First you had to pass the guards outside of the cells and dormitory, then walk through open ground to the metal gate, then out, or otherwise scale the two-meter stone wall circling the compound, with crushed glass bottles and barbed wire on top. If you survived that, you had to run across the twenty-meter fireguard around the compound, hoping the snipers in the watchtower didn't see you and pick you off before you got into the woods.

The odds against anyone escaping were overwhelming.

Many had tried to escape. All had failed. Their bodies and skeletons were left to rot in the open, a warning to those who wanted to attempt to do as they had. Even if one escaped, they wouldn't survive the treacherous forest known as a habitat for the world's most venomous snakes and wild animals. There were more poisonous berries and fruits than edibles. Colette knew that even if she got out she would not survive an escape attempt. And where would she go? One side of the compound was shielded by a river half a mile wide.

More so, Colette could not expect any help. Many of the villagers, even those at a great distance, were terrified of Mubarak. He had been known to wipe out whole families for the transgressions of a single family member. Most of the villagers were bootlickers, and often spied on each other. Some secretly worked for him, ratting out anyone who spoke ill of him, in exchange for favors. Locals claimed he had eyes everywhere. They nicknamed him "The Eagle," a moniker Mubarak adopted for himself.

In the camp, crime was forbidden, often receiving severe punishment. The presence of children and adults with half-limbs was a reminder. The punishment for stealing was loss of an arm, or the hand used to steal. Prisoners were thrown into the cells behind the garage, or beneath it, a windowless dungeon with a damp dirt floor. Next to it was where the sick and injured were kept. Mubarak was the supreme judge, leaving petty crimes to be resolved by his trusted minions who carried out his will across the region.

The most secure building was Mubarak's home —the mansion. A French Renaissance style-chateau, it had thirty bedrooms and thirty-five bathrooms. Flowering gardens and hedgerows and finally a brick wall artfully surrounded it, with several curved, symmetrical stone pathways leading from the main house into the garden, where there were several koi ponds and water fountains. Armed guards patrolled the grounds around the clock. There was an equestrian facility where several of his thoroughbred horses were kept. Farther away were caged tigers and lions that Mubarak kept as pets. He had a fleet of more than forty vehicles including several Rolls-Royces and G-wagons that he sometimes drove here and there. While every other building in the compound had asbestos roofing, the mansion was the only building in the compound with ceramic tile roofing. Eastward from the mansion, but not within sight, were factories where gold and diamonds were processed and sorted. A solar farm, also not visible from the grounds, supplied off-the-grid electricity when needed to power the security fence and gates.

Most of his guards and soldiers had been groomed from childhood, having been abducted or forcibly taken from their parents. There were a few parents who believed Mubarak to be some deity, and willingly gave up some of their children, as young as four years old, to serve him. Every morning the children were forced to recite chosen texts and sing Mubarak's anthem:

All hail Mubarak!
All hail the chosen!
Long live the Eagle!

They were on a constant propaganda diet until they were brainwashed, and the young men underwent grueling physical training, so that by the time they were released into the world nothing would stop them from pleasing their father and hating the world as a filthy place that needed cleansing. Everyone in the compound called him Father.

Several boys were chosen from all the children that came into the compound's training camp for the special assignments team, the elite team. Qualification for this was brutal, marking a transition from boyhood not to manhood, but into a killing machine. The selection happened between ages ten to fourteen. Those chosen for special assignments were sent out into the forest to hunt a gorilla using only bare hands and brains. They were not allowed to return to the camp without a gorilla's head; to do so was punishable by death. The majority never returned from the treacherous jungle. The few who did were respected and sat at their father's feet.

Some of the children not chosen for the elite team became soldiers or guards. They maintained order and made sure the lithium, gold, diamond, sulphur, and platinum miners' daily quotas and weekly targets were met, by any means necessary. Some soldiers were trained kidnappers and hostage-takers.

The rest, referred to as lowlings, became workers. Children and people from the nearby villages worked in the mines. Some volunteered to do so and some were forced. Mubarak had violated all human rights known to mankind. To him, human rights were a mere suggestion. He made his own rules—a god in the region. Everyone feared him. The international community had done nothing to unseat him because he was feeding their coffers with gold, diamonds, platinum, sulphur, and lithium, mined by workers served one meal per day, often cornmeal and vegetables from the big compound garden. The equatorial weather allowed vegetables to grow throughout the year. Laborers worked six and a half days a week, dawn until dusk. Those who died in the mines were buried in a pit. The other half-day of the week was reserved for performing services around the mansion. While everyone else toiled, it was rumored that all of Mubarak's fifteen children, by ten different women, were studying at prestigious universities in Singapore, Switzerland, France, the U.K., and the U.S.A.

AMONG THE FEW who completed the gorilla quest and managed to leave the compound was Karim. Karim had been born in the compound, to a housemaid in Mubarak's palace. There were rumors Mubarak had raped her, as was often the case, although he had twelve wives. As an illegitimate son, Karim was ostracized based on the local customs, hence at first not treated as a son. The boy grew up shifty and devious, and quick to anger. But Mubarak saw himself in young Karim. He paid trainers secretly to teach the boy to fight. He never acknowledged his mother or spoke her name. The boy proved to be a killing machine, better than anyone Mubarak had seen. He was Mubarak's protégé. At the age of fourteen, Karim was sent to study in France. It was while he was in France, by mistake having put on a friend's eyeglasses in class, that he realized he was nearsighted. Since then he had worn eyeglasses.

He believed his mission was to please his father and further his father's greatness. As a strong believer, the kid had succeeded, even managing to join the French foreign brigade until it was time for his long-awaited mission. When his father called, he answered. Earning his father's approval and acceptance became his reason for existing. He ought to be the best at whatever was asked of him. His destiny was to kill and eliminate whatever and whoever his father requested.

Karim had been sent on numerous special missions to kill. Presidents, opposition leaders, governors, and legislators were all on his resume. His subordinates did suicide bombings and abductions as directed, thwarting dissent among workers and villagers, or keeping law enforcement in line: work that was beneath him. Yet he had spent his whole life dedicated, awaiting the message his father promised he would one day receive, to carry out one very important mission.

CHAPTER
THIRTY-THREE

AT DUSK, the child laborers returned to their cells at Mubarak's compound. Colette and her friends, Judith and Priscilla, had spent the whole day in the cell. A guard later brought in a trolley of food. He shoved three metal plates beneath the heavy metal bars of their cell. The guard moved on to the next cell where several child laborers were being held. He gave these children less food, a limited variety. The guard moved on down the line of cells.

Colette bit into her slice of bread. She watched her friend Judith, who bawled as she lay on the dirt floor, ignoring the food.

"You need to eat. You'll need your strength. We don't know how long we will be in this."

Judith sobbed. "What's the point? We are going to die."

"No, they will not kill us. They need something from my father."

Colette stood up and sneaked in a slice of bread through the bars to the thin little boy in the cell beside theirs. The boy took the bread and smiled at

Colette. She returned and sat next to Priscilla and Judith.

"We need to devise a way to escape."

"Escape? Do you even know where we are?"

"No, but we still have to try. What if my dad doesn't find us?"

"We can't go anywhere. Look at these chains," Priscilla said.

"We need to find something sharp to pick open the lock-pads."

Judith said, "It's all dirt and concrete in here. I don't see anywhere we can find anything to pick the locks."

"If we can get the chains off, we can get out," Colette said.

"We're never going to make it far. They will shoot us. You saw how many guards are around this place."

"You don't know that."

"I know how to use a gun," Colette said. "If one of us gets out, maybe they can get help. Then we can help the children here."

"How can we get the keys from the guards? The keys hang around their necks."

"I don't know. But we will find a way."

The girls hushed when they heard the guard's footsteps approaching. The guard returned to his post next to their cell, sat, and started eating his meal.

The boy in the next cell stood up and walked to the bars. He lifted his eyes from the bread he was eating and pointed at the guard.

Colette eyes followed the boy's finger. "Genius!" she said.

"What?" both Judith and Priscilla said at the same time.

"Hit me!" Colette told Priscilla.

"What? I can't—"

Colette slapped Priscilla and interrupted her. Confused, Priscilla launched at Colette and the two girls tussled on the dirt floor, rolling and yelling.

The guard, seeing this, stood up and approached the cell.

"Stop, you brats! I see you're not hungry!"

He opened the door and approached to peel the two girls from each other. Colette charged at the guard, causing him to drop the bowl and teaspoon on the ground. Some of the bean soup spilled on his uniform. He cursed and slapped Colette.

"You're lucky the boss wants you unharmed! If you do that again, you're dead!"

The guard picked up his empty bowl, and their plates with food, and locked the metal door behind himself. He used a cloth to wipe off the stain on his uniform. The stain remained. He knew Mubarak wanted all uniforms crisp and clean.

Cursing, he stormed down the tunnel.

Priscilla stared at Colette. Colette smiled.

"What was that for?" Priscilla said.

"Jackpot!" she said, raising the copper teaspoon in her hand.

"That was your plan?"

"Yes."

"That's not gonna fit into the lock!"

"I know. We will sharpen the spoon handle using the rough concrete walls. It will take time, but it will work."

"Are you sure?"

"Watch and learn."

"Have you picked a lock before?"

"Many times. My dad and Joel, my bodyguard, taught me."

Colette went to work.

THIRTY-FOUR

AFTER RECEIVING A MESSAGE FROM OPHÉLIE, the jet took a detour to Mombasa, where Six and Reggie were to meet Ophélie. They arrived at Moi International Airport early in the morning and took a taxi towards their rendezvous. They drove past the beautiful Mombasa train terminus as the Madaraka Express train was pulling into the Kenyan port city in from Nairobi. The railway was part of the decade-long East African Railway Network project funded by loans from China.

"This is nice," Six said.

"It is. But it's all on borrowed money. Some phases are still incomplete farther west, stalled due to financial negotiations."

"You say that like it's a bad thing."

"It's good. But most of these contracts are screwing future generations."

"Hey, they gotta live for now, right? Screw the future, as long as the politicians look good right now."

"What would you expect after years and years

of incentivizing poverty? I think all this foreign aid and social welfare does more harm than good."

"I see Chris's viewpoint," Reggie added. "As a collective union, the continent can easily pay those loans quickly."

The taxi dropped them off in front of a Mediterranean restaurant. Ophélie was already at the restaurant. Once seated, Six ordered the lamb shank, Reggie the chicken kabob. Ophélie went for the gyros platter. They all ordered the napoleon for dessert from a comprehensive list that included both Mediterranean and French pastries, and local favorites. The server brought the food.

"Eating like a man," Six said, sinking his teeth into the shank.

Reggie raised her eyebrows.

Six wiped his mouth with a paper towel. "I feel like a Viking eating this massive piece of tender goodness."

They all laughed.

"What are you doing here?" Reggie said.

"Many things," Ophélie said. "Some of which I can't tell you. I have info that might interest you, detective. My source gave info on the Triple Z smuggling rout here in Mombasa."

"It's been on our radar for a while. We know it's one of the main smuggling routes for cocaine from South America to Europe, Asia, and the Middle East."

"Now you add Triple Z into the mix," Six said.

"Yeah. A multi-billion-dollar industry."

"Still a lot of work to be done."

Reggie said to Ophélie, "How long do you plan to be here?"

"One more day. I've a few more people to convince around here. I will see you guys in Addis Ababa on the twenty-fourth."

"You're missing out on the fun," Six said.

"My job is not guns and crime scenes. I make people do things."

Six smirked. "You manipulate them."

"You could say that. It's an art," Ophélie said, flipping her hair back.

"Any progress finding Colette?"

"We are getting close. Where do you start looking in a country of over sixty million people?"

"We are here for the Tangier murder," Six said. "What do you have for us about the murder in Tangier or Colette?"

"I found a guy who has intel for you," Ophélie said.

"Helpful information?"

"He claims he knows who is behind the assassination in Tangier and the attacks. Claims he has been part of the squad as well."

"How do you know this whistleblower? What do you know about our guy?" Six said.

"I have my ways. He is an Arab guy. Met him two days ago in Tangier at a bar."

"How?"

"I was there at the hotel when the assassination happened, waiting to meet and convince the delegate to sign the document—"

"The decoy?" Reggie said.

"Yes. But he didn't know he was being used as bait. And I saw a man I thought I recognized. A man wearing glasses. So I asked around."

"I have seen a guy like that before," Six said. "But it could be anyone."

"How do we get to this guy who has intel?" Reggie said.

"My contact will meet you in Tangier. He has information that will help."

"Where do we meet him?"

"He will find you. Go to this place." Ophélie handed a note to Six with a name.

"What is this?"

"It's a shop. Ask around, you will find it. Be there tonight at 9:00 p.m. He will find you."

Six and Reggie left the restaurant and took a taxi back to the airport. The jet took off for Morocco.

SIX AND REGGIE checked into their hotel rooms at the Dar Chams Tanja hotel off the Mediterranean coast in Tangier just as the muezzin's call to prayer echoed through the streets. They paid thirty dollars cash for each room, no identification needed. They immediately went up to the rooftop terrace for the beautiful view overlooking the city.

Once refreshed, they headed out. The crime scene was a few blocks away from their hotel. They decided to walk. The beach town's landscape was craggy, with steep hills and narrow streets and alleys. The cobblestone streets were packed with pedestrians and vendors.

The coastline was lined with colorful houses creating a tapestry of traditional Arab and Berber architecture with old French, English, German, and Spanish influences, reminiscent of the country's colonial past.

There were visible attempts at gentrification. Yet the city maintained its old-time charm. Redolent of past times was the Arabic architecture ornamented with tiles in Islamic patterns.

They arrived at the Royal Tulip hotel where the murder had taken place, showed their badges, and asked for the manager. The concierge scrutinized their badges. He led them past the lobby to an office. The manager was a short, staunch man dressed in a white robe, an ornamented vest, and a red Igbo cap.

"The local police have already been all over us," the manager said.

He led them up to the floor where the murder had occurred. The hall was draped with yellow police tape. Six and Reggie dodged below the yellow "no trespassing" tape. Nothing in the room had been disturbed, and where the body had been lying a few days earlier the bedsheets were undone.

They returned to his office.

"Do you have any video footage from that day?"

"Yes. We have copies. We gave the originals to the local police."

"Copies will work."

The manager played a video from his desktop computer. Six pointed to a woman. They both could see Ophélie in a red dress at the counter in the lobby.

"You know her?" the manager said.

"A colleague."

"Keep playing?" He sped up the video.

They watched for twenty minutes. Then Six paused it. The man wearing glasses was leaving the elevator. He had made sure to keep his head tilted downward and avoid direct eye contact with the cameras, seeming to know exactly where they were.

"That's him."

"Can we run facial recognition?"

"Good luck from that angle," Reggie said. "There is no way. The guy knew it would be impossible."

"But he is our guy."

"Do you remember seeing this guy?"

The manager strained to think and closed his eyes.

"I'm sorry, I cannot remember any one guest. I see hundreds of people a day. Unless they are regular customers, I don't remember."

"Show us the list of guests checked in for that night."

"Here is a list of guests we had on the second and third floors that night."

"There is nothing suspicious," said Reggie.

"He obviously used a fake name," said Six. "Or if he is a professional, someone else bought the room for him. Do you take cash?" he asked the manager.

The manager hesitated. "Yes, sometimes."

Six and Reggie exchanged glances.

The manager squirmed in his seat. "Please, you must understand. Times are tough. Taxes are high. We must do what we can to survive."

"What you do with your taxes is your problem right now. I think our guy paid in cash."

"But how would he get access to the third floor? That's the royal suite. You need an I.D. clearance to get in."

"That's easy for professionals."

"It's evident he used an employee's badge."

"We checked the scan records. None of our employees entered that area at that time of night. It was only the victim's I.D."

"Then our murderer used the target's badge."

"How is that even possible?" the manager said.

"Not impossible to do," Six said.

Six studied some of the photographs of the victim. He said, "The marks on the neck show this was a deliberate murder. They were not trying to hide it. Whoever did this wanted us to know."

AFTER THE MURDER SCENE, Six and Reggie arrived at the Petit Socco, a small market square within the city's Medina quarter, as the sun was setting. The square was bustling with people for early evening. They were greeted with aromas wafting from the street food: spices, herbs, fresh bread, coffee. They evaded two hustlers who tried to get money from them for recommending the best café in the area. Six refused, and the men backed off. The agents ascended the narrow, winding streets, passing several traditional craftsmanship items on display in front of shops full of them.

Six and Reggie chose an ancient café, made of whitewashed bricks, on the high ground overlooking the streets below, where they could see most of the square and the Mediterranean.

Six ordered black coffee and Reggie the organic Moroccan mint green tea.

The inside whistleblower had requested to meet near here based on the note from Ophélie. A good choice, since it was a crowded place. They still had thirty minutes before the rendezvous. At 8:00 p.m., Six and Reggie descended the narrow alley and met the guy behind a food stall, which they found by asking the locals for directions.

They arrived at the spot and the Arab guy, in blue jeans, a leather jacket, a collared blue shirt, and sneakers, beckoned them behind the stall, in the shadows. He looked disheveled and shaken. His clothes had some dirt spots all over and the shirt smelled.

Six offered a handshake. The man refused. Six smirked at the snub.

"Alright then. Let's get down to business."

The man kept rocking from side to side, eyeing the area to the left, then the right, as if thinking someone was watching him. He kept his back to the wall and his hands inside his jacket pockets. Six kept his eyes on the man's eyes, easing his hand onto the SIG in his pocket for any sudden, possibly betraying movements.

The man looked flustered, fidgety, maybe was on some illegal drugs or over-the counter drugs. His skin was pale, visible even in the dim light.

"You're not the police, are you?"

"No," Six said.

"You have my money?" the man said.

Reggie showed him a hundred-dollar bill but did not give it to him. The man tried to take it.

"Tell us what you know, and you'll have your money."

"How do I know you will keep your word?"

"Depends on what you tell us. Who killed the delegate at the hotel?" Six said.

"I don't know. But I think I know the people involved."

"Tell us."

"I was part of the Nettoyer Brigade of the Foreign Legion. They called us the cleaners, *les nettoyer*. I was a field analyst for the operation but spent some time on the ground."

"Where were you born?" Six said.

"Algeria. It didn't matter. The French army is mostly all kinds of nationalities. Africans, Asians, Arabs."

"Why are you telling us this?"

"We did some crazy stuff in the Republic of the Congo and the Democratic Republic of the Congo. I just want a clear conscience, if that's even possible for me."

"Tell us what you know."

"I think I know the man behind the killing. His name is Karim."

"How do you know this Karim?"

"We were part of the same Legion. This guy—this guy was crazy. Most of us killed based on orders we were following. Karim did it for sport. He is one of those guys that enjoys killing. He went above and beyond what the orders were.

"After the program was terminated, most of us got out, but I heard Karim continued killing. As a contractor. Even forming his own little company of killers."

"Where are the rest of your team?"

"Dead. Last I heard, I'm the only one left. And Karim."

"Does this Karim have a last name?"

"I don't know, man," he said. "We called him Karim in the force. That's all I know. Don't know if it was even his real name."

Six nodded.

"I'm scared, man."

"You are safe here. That's why you chose this place, right?"

"Yes. Yes. You sure you were not followed?"

"No," Reggie said.

"Be careful. This is dangerous. These people are dangerous. I can't keep doing this," the man said.

Reggie handed him the money. He snatched it and stuffed it into his pants pocket and vanished into the dark.

Six and Reggie left the food stall and joined a bunch of pedestrians along the Medina, the stone-cobbled path between stalls of food, spices, and crafts vendors.

CHAPTER
THIRTY-SEVEN

THE ARAB BOUGHT several pouches of Triple Z using the money Reggie had given him in exchange for the information, and got off the bus a few blocks from where he lived. The urge for the drug was intense. He couldn't wait to get home. He would relish the moment he eased into his bathtub and pumped himself with the drug. Bliss.

He trudged along fast, checking from side to side. The paranoia had not left him since his days in the French brigade. He felt it. A sixth sense. Someone from an intersection was following him: a man in an overcoat and a fedora, and glasses. He walked faster. But the man was gaining on him. He wished it was a few years back, when he could have easily killed the people who made him nervous, but his body was frail from alcohol and drug use. He trembled, turned down a dark alley, and sprinted as fast as his sick heart would carry him. With one more right turn he would be inside his house, lock the door, and might have a fighting chance.

He froze when he saw the same man in the

overcoat and hat standing at the end of the alley like the Grim Reaper. He stuffed his hands in his jacket pockets, backed away slowly. His legs felt weak.

"Hello, old friend," the man said. The Arab recognized the voice.

"Karim?" Backing away, he toppled a trash bag that spilled out onto the ground.

"It's been a long time, hasn't it, my brother?"

"What do you want?"

"Nothing, Clément. I want nothing."

By this time the man wearing glasses had closed the distance between them and they were a few feet apart. They stopped moving.

Karim said, "We were brothers once," and shot his former colleague in the chest twice. His legs gave in and he crumpled to the ground. Karim squatted next to the man. He looked at the pleading eyes as a pool of blood formed beneath him.

"You pig!" Karim said. "You betrayed all that our father taught us, for the enemy! For that you deserve to die." Karim wiped his nose, spit, and looked back into the man's eyes. "You did this to yourself. We could have done big things ... you and I. Now you will die here like a dog."

He stood up and left.

THIRTY-EIGHT

SIX AND REGGIE returned to the Royal Tulip hotel. Reggie went upstairs to review the crime scene. Six lingered in the lobby, pretending to read a magazine while checking for any signs of danger.

Six's phone rang. It was Reggie.

"Are you coming up? Where are you?" Reggie said.

"I'm in the lobby. Observing people."

"The forensics team is almost done here. I will join you shortly."

"Let me get back to you. There's something I need to check."

"What is it?" said Reggie.

"I will explain later."

"What is it?"

"I gotta go!"

"Six! Six! Dammit!" Reggie left the bathroom, which she was investigating, and ran to the balcony. She saw Six vanishing into the crowds, running.

Six had recognized in the lobby the suspect from the Safari Club. Their eyes locked. The man bolted out of the hotel lobby and disappeared among the throngs of people. Six followed him for three blocks, where the man got into a Peugeot 308 parked down the street three blocks from the hotel, a driver in the car and the engine running. The vehicle screeched off.

Six sprinted across the street after the Peugeot. He skipped past one block, catching a glimpse of the Peugeot disappearing around the corner. He flagged a car, pointed his handgun, and ordered the driver out. The driver obliged. Six rammed the vehicle into drive, full throttle. The chase continued across downtown, up and down the hill, narrowly missing collisions. A few blocks in, Six heard a crack: a gunshot. Then the Peugeot in front of him skidded across the road, flipped twice, and crashed into a utility pole. Six caught up seconds later. He dashed to the vehicle, now upside down. The driver had been shot in the head and had been killed instantly. The man on the passenger side screamed in pain. "Help me!" he said.

Another "crack" sounded, this time on the other side. "Shit!" cried Six, and rolled behind the car while another sniper shot we through the man's chest. Blood spattered the windshield on the passenger side. Six paused to gauge where the bullet had come from. *Could be from anywhere in these buildings*, he thought. The wounded man muttered some words. Six did not know what the phrases meant. The man repeated the phrases.

Six reached for the door and tried to uncinch the wounded man's seat belt. It was slippery with blood. The seatbelt was stuck, would not release him. The man held onto Six and he gurgled words, blood clogging his mouth.

"They are not going to stop!"

Six pressed the man's torso to slow down the arterial blood spray, while crouching as low as possible.

"Who is 'they'?"

"The charter. They want it."

"What charter? You mean the—"

The man gripped Six's shirt. "Find it before they do, or they will keep on killing. All hail the chosen! Long live the Eagle!"

Six struggled to undo the seatbelt. Six gave up, searched for the man's phone, took it, and pressed the man's forefinger onto the power button. The phone unlocked.

Then came the kill shot. The bullet shattered the windshield, knocked the man backward, left a hole in his head, and embedded itself into the fabric of the headrest. He died instantly. His arms dropped to his sides and hung loose. Six jumped behind the car, looking in both directions. He rolled back and darted to the side, staying as low to the ground as he could. Another shot rang out, puncturing a tire. Then two more, puncturing three tires. Then another shot directly hit the fuel tank. Then the bullets stopped. Six scooted off into the darkest shadows he could find.

Six now knew someone was watching him and was sending a clear message.

He wondered who. He returned to the hotel. Reggie had been right to do more investigation. He ought to review what had been found.

CHAPTER
THIRTY-NINE

KARIM WAS SUPPOSED to be out of town by now, but his subordinates had failed. Word had reached him that the airport attack had failed. He was always the one to face the heat from Father and clean up the subordinates' messes.

It had been two days now since the Tangier hotel assassination, and despite the hordes of local police flooding the hotel, they found nothing tied to Karim. He checked his fitness tracker. He still had two hours before his flight. He double-checked the closet, snapped his backpack on and walked out of the Four Seasons hotel room and the hotel. He walked along the boulevard. His jacket felt thin in the cold front that had come in that evening. But that was okay. He hoped his flight would not be canceled or delayed.

He waited by the lamppost, watching flying termites clustered around the lamp, and finally flagged a taxi. He resisted the urge to stop at the casino a few kilometers down the road at the Mövenpick hotel. His temper usually ended him in trouble in places like these. He took the taxi to his favorite coffee shop at a café near the top of the hill, overlooking the hotel where he had been a few days earlier.

Outside, people were celebrating. The street was packed with droves of people in green and red t-shirts and flags, all soccer fans, some drunk. Chanting "Go Atlas Lion, go!" It was the night of the World Cup. Karim had watched the sport occasionally, and knew Morocco had a reputation for going deep into the tournament. He was proud for a moment although he had never been a fan, except in his old college frat days. He was thankful he had left that life at age twenty-two. The taxi waited for the pedestrians to pass. He didn't mind, enjoyed the long ride. His stomach grumbled; he was famished. His regular use of Triple Z had made his appetite skyrocket so at that instant he was sure he could eat a whole goat. The bearded driver played some good Moroccan folk music. Karim tipped the driver and found a seat next to the window in the restaurant which had a view of the city center and the Royal Tulip hotel. He perused the menu, even though he already knew what he wanted. He ordered "the country dinner." A bowl of tomato-basil soup, two double cheeseburgers, and large order of French fries arrived shortly. He found American food very tasty. It always left him wanting more. Just the right amount of excess fat, sugar, and salt for his unrefined palate. He told himself he would scotch all the calories when he went to the gym. He washed it all down with a large latte. He ordered a second large latte and sat on the straw chair listening to local musicians, a husband and wife on the harp and keyboard. The beautiful, traditional folk music—

peaceful, yet with such emotion. The music carried him. At that moment, everything was perfect. Then his phone buzzed. It was his guy from the Royal Tulip hotel, his "eyes." The "eyes" were working there and said to him, "The investigators are here."

Karim decided to have a chat with Six. He phoned the hotel manager's number. It rang twice. The receptionist answered and transferred the phone to Six, who was in the manager's office reviewing hotel registries, employee records, and files. Six waved it away and motioned for Reggie to take it.

Reggie pressed the receiver onto her ear. "Detective Kona."

"Detective? What a pleasure," the voice said with a coarse French accent.

"Who's this?"

"Nobody. Can I talk to your boyfriend? Or should I say Agent Six?"

"Who are you?"

"Someone you should not be fucking with? Give me the document. Get out of my way or I'll keep killing."

"You know I can't do that."

"Now give the phone to Agent Six. He and I had a showdown earlier this evening. Agent Six, I know you can hear me."

Reggie put the phone on speaker.

"Who's this?" said Six.

"Surprise, surprise," Karim said. "We meet again after our earlier showdown. I decided to introduce myself."

"Karim," Six said.

There was a pause on the other end. "Oh, I see you have done your homework!"

"I'm going to find you," Six said. "And I'm going to kill you!"

Karim laughed hysterically.

"I let you live tonight. Next time we meet, I won't be lenient with my bullets."

"That's too bad," Six said. "I'm going to kill you."

"I'll do the same. How ironic. See you around."

The phone call ended.

CHAPTER
FORTY

SIX'S OTHER phone was not a regular phone, but a special communication device capable of scrambling messages so that only a specific code could open them. Six had heard the phone's number was constantly changing. Communication was simple. He hit the red dial and asked a question. Someone answered and information was sent to his phone's screen. Just like that. This was the phone reserved for communicating with his handler and relaying classified information.

Six decided not to tell Reggie or the local team about what he had heard the dying man say. Instead he phoned his handler and relayed the phrases. He forwarded the files he had downloaded from the man's phone to his handler, and also forwarded photos of the Peugeot, the two dead men and the fingerprints of the phone's owner, which Six had extracted from the phone's home button.

"Hey, Six," the handler's voice said.

"Hey, Jackie, I need to run through some new information with you."

"What do you have?" she said.

"Could not understand what the guy was saying when he was dying. He kept repeating some words and phrases several times."

"Do you remember the words?" she said.

"All hail the chosen! Long live the Eagle!"

"Let me see what I can dig up."

Next, Six phoned Lin, an MI6 agent, part of the MI6's international operation counterintelligence team. Several months before, Lin had tracked a shipping container full of trafficked girls, all the way to Victoria Falls, where she met Six while they were both investigating the same target for different crimes. She, Reggie, and Six had then worked together to clamp down on a human trafficking syndicate that ran all the way from Shanghai to Vic Falls.

Lin did not answer. But seconds later Six's phone rang.

Lin spoke, "Hey big guy. Long time."

"Deliberating about whether to flake on my call?" Six said.

Lin laughed. "No. That would be too much mental space which I don't have. You aren't that important."

"Thank goodness. I'd be worried. Better use that tiny brain of yours for something worthwhile."

"Okay, Mr. Philosopher. What do you want?"

"I need a favor?"

"Depends on what you want."

Six relayed the phrases from the dead man to Lin and forwarded the fingerprints and photos.

"I know you guys have tentacles that span all over the globe."

"Not quite."

"Just help me out, okay?"

"I'll see what I can do," she said.

"Thanks, Lin."

"Don't thank me yet."

"One more question. Are these your guys behind the attacks across Africa?"

"I guarantee you we are not in the least involved in this," Lin said.

Six could tell she was telling the truth.

"If it was our guys, I'd know."

"And you would tell me?"

"I wouldn't. But this makes me sick also. Big British companies have investments in countries that are being disrupted by the attacks. That's why I know it's not us."

"I believe you."

"We have moved on from the empire and monarch days. At least we don't use guns to claim territories now."

"Point taken."

"I'll get back to you when I find something."

SIX AND REGGIE were back in Addis Ababa at 9:00 the next morning. They felt refreshed after sleeping on the full-size beds in the jet throughout the seven-hour direct flight from Tangier. Six went for a long jog. It allowed him to think. Reggie had decided to stay at their small hotel in downtown Addis Ababa to write a progress report for the Bureau. Six took the long way home, passing through alleys into the city's quieter corners with local pubs and makeshift food markets. There was also the possibility he might get some information from a drunkard.

He received a phone call from an unknown caller.

"Agent Six," the altered voice said. "Our paths collide again."

"Karim."

"That works as well. Let me let you on a little secret."

Six listened and switched on the call-tracking widget.

"Remember the airport attack? If I had wanted

Mr. Mussa to die, I could have killed him before you arrived. Why would I allow the medics to get the injured into an ambulance just in time for you to rescue him?"

"And why are you telling me this?"

"Being a friend."

"I gotta go."

"Uh-uh. Let's just say conditions are changing. And for that to happen, you need to stay out of my way."

"You know I can't do that."

"Then when the time comes, I'll have to kill you."

"I'll die trying," Six said. "I will find you."

"Get out of my way," the voice said. "You are starting to be a pain in my ass. Don't say I didn't warn you. I'm going to start killing your friends."

The call ended. Exactly fifty-nine seconds. Whoever called knew Six would be tracking the call.

The voice had sounded familiar.

Six called Reggie immediately. The phone rang once.

"Reggie, where are you?"

"In my hotel room. Why?"

"Had another call from Karim, I think. Making sure you're safe. He was threatening."

A chill went down Reggie's spine. "I'm fine." She walked to the window and looked outside, then drew the curtains.

"I'm thirty minutes away," said Six.

"I'm fine—."

That's when Reggie heard them. Her heart leaped.

"They are here! I gotta go!" she whispered.

She hung up. She could feel the adrenalin coursing through her veins.

The polished wooden floor squeaked. Several footsteps. Three, maybe four people in heavy combat boots were approaching her room. They stopped at the door, then fiddled with its lock. Reggie scrambled to retrieve her gun from the nightstand, checking that the silencer was attached, then slid behind the bed. After several deep breaths, she took aim at the door. The lock clicked, and then the door opened, slowly. She waited. Counted. Three men wearing body armor aimed at the bed. Reggie fired three rounds, each into and out of each of their heads. The men collapsed to the floor one after another. Reggie waited. There were no more sounds. She tiptoed quickly towards the door.

The fourth man, who had stayed in the hallway, saw her, barged into the room through the gaping doorway, and with one brilliant sweep of his arm knocked Reggie's gun away from her, grabbed it and aimed it at her. Reggie spun and kicked him with such force that it knocked the pistol out of the man's hands. She grabbed the artificial fern wreath that hung on the door and lunged towards the man, knocked him down and wound the wreath around the man's neck. He gulped for air. His eyes bulged like white golf balls, almost popping out of his skull, pleading for dear life. She pulled the wreath more tightly. The wire sank into the man's flesh, ripping his life away. Reggie let go, and the man lay motionless on the carpet with the others. Reggie trembled. Her body flushed hot.

She checked the hallway, both ends and stairwells. She looked out the window, up and down the street. There was no one. She drew the curtains, locked her door and called the police.

Shortly afterward, the place around the hotel was filled with squad cars and sirens as several police officers arrived. For the next hour, as the four bodies and shell casings were measured and photographed, Reggie answered questions from the local police and a homicide detective. The paramedic's evaluation showed she needed only antibacterial ointment and a bandage to her elbow and forearm, and a band-aid on her face. The police promised to investigate the perpetrators and their motivation, speculating that they probably attempted armed robbery. Privately, Reggie was skeptical. She did not have expensive items with her, nor was she wearing jewelry or clothes suggesting that she might have more valuables in her room. If they were only thieves, they could have broken in when she was not there and avoided the risk of an armed confrontation. Professional thieves in forty-five seconds would have broken into and stripped every room on the floor, and then ran. But her assailants had been wearing body armor, expecting a confrontation. Why target her room and not any others, unless she herself was the target?

Six arrived shortly afterward. He brought hot chocolate and had Reggie move into his room for the night. Six took the couch and let Reggie have the bed. They talked.

"The caller's accent is the same," Six said. "But his voice is always altered."

"Could be a robo call. A.I. nowadays, it's becoming hard to tell what's real or not."

"I think I saw Karim when we rescued Mussa.

He had a rifle aimed at the ambulance, but let us go."

"Why would he do that? Toying with us?"

Six sat up, remembering what the caller had said. "I think we led him to the document. That's what he wanted all along."

"What?"

"Call Chris."

Six and Reggie phoned Chris. No answer. They tried again and again. Still no answer.

CHAPTER
FORTY-TWO

THE LAND CRUISER blazed through the streets of Addis Ababa towards the Osage estate. It screeched to a halt a few yards outside of Chris's home. Six and Reggie jumped out, guns at the ready, and sprinted towards the main gate. The guard there let them in, surprised.

"Detective, what is wrong?"

"Where is Chris?"

"Mr. Osage is in the main house. Is—?"

Reggie and Six had already bolted toward the house before he could finish speaking.

Nothing outside of the house seemed to have been disturbed. Six and Reggie inside the house kept very quiet and swept their guns from side to side. There was no movement or sound. Then they heard a sound. They aimed.

"Crap! It's M.J." Chris's dog scampered across the lawn towards them from the hedges, skidded across the polished flooring, stopped and then trotted ahead of them. The agents advanced, sweeping through each room, following the dog.

M.J. led them to the study. Chris and Sheila

were there, tied to a heavy sofa and with mouths, wrists, and ankles taped. Reggie peeled the tape from their mouths.

"Who did this?"

"The driver from the ambulance."

"How did he free himself?"

"I don't know."

"Does he have the document?"

"No. He tried," Chris said, wiping clotted blood from the side of his mouth. "Tortured me and tied us to the chairs, asking for the safe's passcode. It's an old-school safe, with no electronics that can be hacked. Knocked me unconscious."

"He threatened us," said Sheila.

"Where is Tali and the rest of your security detail?"

"In Cape Town," Chris told them. "Hurry. Go help Mussa. He is the one they want. If Mussa is dead, the declaration will be hard to pass. They know this."

"Where is he?"

"Still in the infirmary."

The agents finished freeing the couple. They left the room and continued their sweep towards the infirmary.

They saw first the two guards lying on the ground motionless outside the infirmary.

Mussa was lying on the floor of his room. The intravenous drips had been removed. Reggie checked his pulse. She nodded to Six; Mussa was still alive but barely breathing. They noticed the bullet wound in his right thigh.

"Mr. Mussa, Mr. Mussa!" Six called to him. To Reggie he said, "Where the hell are the nurses?"

"Shh! Shut it! Quiet!"

They crept down a hallway to the office and saw a keypad by its door; it was locked. Reggie shot the keypad off the wall and they kicked the door in and entered shooting. A laptop computer crashed to the floor and they saw the ambulance driver slouched in the office chair, his arms dangling and his head hanging to the side, froth around his mouth. They approached him with guns aimed.

"Dammit. He killed himself. I bet he took a cyanide when he heard us."

"He knew we'd shoot him on sight."

"This all exactly what Karim wanted," Reggie said. "We have totally played into his plot. He didn't kill Mussa at the airport because he knew we'd be told to bring Mussa to where the document is. So we have. And if he didn't get it he could kill Mussa."

"But he has neither Mussa nor the document so far."

"As far as we know. This guy accessed something from those computers."

"We need to find out what he sent."

They rushed back to Mussa's room and did what they could to awaken and bandage him, but he needed more than first aid. They phoned Chris, who from the house was able to remotely free the nurse and aides from the infirmary's safe room where they had locked themselves in.

Six and Reggie spent the rest of the day and most of the night in Chris's home office trying to access the computer files the ambulance driver had sent, before heading back to Six's hotel room.

CHAPTER
FORTY-THREE

JOYCE PHONED at 6:00 a.m. Six had just returned from a walk around the block to stretch and loosen the muscles cramped from sleeping on the small couch in his hotel room. Six put her on loudspeaker so Reggie could hear her too.

"Joyce. You're on speaker. Don't you ever sleep?"

"Well, if one of my friends is attacked, I've got to find who did it."

"What's up?"

"Video call me when you get a chance. I found something you might like."

Six glanced at Reggie, who had woken up.

"How about right now?"

"Sure. Whenever you can."

"Give us five minutes."

Joyce hung up. Joyce, still in Johannesburg, was collaborating with the local medical examiner in Addis Ababa.

Six stood up and approached Reggie. "How did you sleep?"

"Fine. Except my body feels like I've been run over by a truck."

"Here. This should do the trick."

He handed Reggie a cup of coffee.

Reggie smiled. "Thank you, Six!" She wrapped her hands around the warm cup.

Six said, "I went over files, reports, and footage from the hotel. But I couldn't find any leads."

Six and Reggie FaceTimed Joyce at 6:10 a.m. Joyce was in the forensics lab, with her white lab coat on.

"Guys, the men who attacked you were on some kind of psychedelic drug," she said.

"Let me guess, Triple Z?" Reggie said.

"That's right. Toxicology results came back positive for Triple Z for all the victims."

"I saw the report you emailed earlier," Reggie said. "The drug is everywhere."

"Could be just druggies hoping for a big kickback. But the way this happened tells me there was some intricate planning. There is a mastermind behind the attack," she said.

"Reggie and I think so too. Closing in on a potential suspect."

"And another thing," Joyce said. "I don't know how important it might be."

"Good news?"

"We know where the mall bombers are from. New forensics data point to pollen from the Congo Basin. Let me share my screen."

Joyce indicated a point on a map. "The pollen on the victim is from a plant found only in the Congo Basin. Once we had that, the biotechs found identical pollen residue on all the crime scenes: in

Joburg, in Vic Falls, in Tangier, and one of the men who attacked Reggie."

"That can't be a coincidence," Reggie said.

"My thoughts exactly. This suggests all these guys have been in the Congo."

"Where in the Congo? Republic or the DRC? Where do you start to search in a country as big as Congo?"

"All this does is it narrows down things a bit."

"So they kidnapped the girls in South Africa, and transported them all the way to Congo. How?"

"Same way traffickers do," Reggie said. "It's big business, and there are a lot of people involved in the chain. Border police, local authorities, smugglers."

"Anything on the DNA?"

"DNA tracing is useless here unless you have a suspect. Here they still work with fingerprints from laser-printed hard copies. Where can we start? These guys are smart enough to not leave any prints anywhere."

"Tell me about it," Reggie said. "None of the guys who attacked my room were identified. All fingerprints were burnt off."

"My friends at the CIA or MI6 might know," Six said. "They know what's going on along the region. They have been monitoring the region for decades."

Six and Reggie thanked Joyce. Joyce reminded Six of the drink he had promised her a year ago after doing them a favor during an earlier investigation. Joyce had not forgotten.

CHAPTER
FORTY-FOUR

SIX AND REGGIE got back to the Osage estate and updated Chris about Joyce's findings, and Chris told them Mussa was in serious condition but would probably not die.

After Six told Reggie about the phrases repeated by the shot man in the car, they stopped by the Abrehot Library and researched for few hours. After forty-five minutes, Reggie went to Six, who was sitting in a carrel with a pile of books and declassified files.

Reggie placed the notepad she was holding on the table.

"The phrases he spoke are a code once used by the notorious Ethiopian assassins against the Italians. In 1896, during the battle of Adwa, Italian forces invaded Ethiopia, but they were defeated by a small, specialized regiment. The regiment used the same phrases, claiming they were divinely inspired to die for the monarch. *'All hail the chosen! Long live the Eagle! Long live the Father!'* It became a hymn."

"So who is the father?"

"Newspapers since the 1990s have claimed that the followers of the crime lord, Mubarak, who terrorized central and eastern Africa since the nineties, used the same phrases. He believed he was some kind of god. Divinely predestined to rule. He has been on our radar for years now. It's making sense now. His followers used the phrases before they committed murders or when dying. Submitting their life to the Father's cause."

"Meaning our Karim and the mall terrorists may be working for this guy?"

"That's a possibility."

"Dang, if I had only killed the guy when I had the chance!"

Six's phone buzzed. It was his handler. Six excused himself and took the call.

"Jackie, what do you have for me?"

"I have updates about the girls."

Six moved to a carrel with a door and shut himself in.

Jackie said, "We are still seeing a time signature from the same location. There is always a back-and-forth communication between a satellite and your smartwatch, even when it's powered off. That's how your time stays correct. Based on that signature, we were able to track one of the girls' fitness trackers using the satellite. Seems as if one of the guys kept a watch he took from Colette's friend. It's been off, but the satellite communication still works regardless."

"The guys don't know that?"

"I doubt it. Unless you do our job, the average person doesn't even know or care that it's happening in the background."

"That's great. Where?"

"In the Republic of the Congo."

"Is there a precise location?"

"Yes. I'm sending you the details now."

A few moments later, an encrypted message notification lit up his phone.

Six updated Reggie. They both decided to leave for the Democratic Republic of the Congo without telling anyone, not even Chris.

FORTY-FIVE

SIX AND REGGIE sat at the airport café, reading a booklet about yellow fever. Six's phone buzzed. An unknown number.

"Are you going to pick that up?" Reggie said.

"No." Six looked at the number and showed the screen to Reggie. Then he rejected the call. The phone buzzed again.

"Only five people in the world have my number," he said to Reggie. "You, my grandmother, and three people from work."

"Could be a robo call."

"No. This phone is encrypted."

"It's a 243 code. That's the Democratic Republic of the Congo. Answer it."

Six answered the call.

"Hey, Six, it's Lin," the voice from the other side said.

Six recognized Lin's voice.

"Why are you using a 243 number? That's the DRC."

"That was the safest way for me to contact you without being tracked."

"Where are you?"

"At an undisclosed location in Africa."

"Specific?"

"You know I can't tell you that," said Lin. "Where are you?"

"Headed to the DRC!"

"What are you doing there?"

"Birdwatching."

Lin said, "The phrases you sent me earlier are from a manifesto by followers of Asan Mubarak."

Six turned to Reggie. "You were right. Lin confirms the phrases." To Lin he said, "That lines up with what we know historically about the phrases and intel that the dead guys had pollen residue from the Congo."

"Then they all have to be from there and they work for Mubarak. Probably he got them as kids and trained them," said Lin.

"That explains why both men got shot when I approached the car."

"We have been after him for over a decade. No one knew where he was exactly. Africa hides fugitives well. You can live completely off-grid for years."

"But justice always catches up to you," said Six.

"Our intel says most of his operations are done by a man named Karim."

Six and Reggie exchanged glances.

Lin continued, "He's a former member of France's foreign legion. Son to Algerian immigrants. They call him 'the shadow,' but his real name is Karim Babouché. Retired. He commanded the brigade that was called 'the cleaners.' After the operation he and several members from his unit went rogue. They kept cleaning. Mainly doing private contracts, particularly in Africa. Our intel reports that several have mysteriously died."

"Why now?

"Maybe they are cleaning the slate. Loose ends. Their boss has been on INTERPOL's most-wanted list for over a decade. Violation of human rights."

"They're finding him only now?"

"Bureaucracy. Also, he has been elusive in the jungle. There was nowhere for us to start. But dictators, eventually they become impulsive. Reckless," Lin said. "Fingerprints from the man shot in the car came back blank from the local police station. Nothing very useful from the files you sent from his phone. They cleaned their trail. He was French, not a local."

"Why would a French assassin be targeting African leaders?"

"You have to ask?"

"I'm not supposed to tell you this. But our intelligence report suggests there was a charter when the African Union was formed in the 1960s. At least there were rumors. A charter where all African leaders signed to make Africa one nation. The French then didn't want that to happen. This charter disappeared. Reports say it has resurfaced and is in the hands of a Mr. Chris, an avid Pan-Africanist and a billionaire who has the resources and influence to push the charter through, single-handedly. And get a Pan-African leader elected. Dictators and corporations will stop at nothing to veto this. There is a fierce opponent well hidden in the Republic of the Congo who calls himself 'Father' and we think it is Mubarak."

"I think we need to pay him a visit."

"I agree. I will meet you guys in Kinshasa. I will send you the rendezvous location."

Six thanked Lin and hung up. He said to Reggie, "MI6 has confirmed everything we know. We have a target."

The airport attendant announced that the flight was boarding. Six and Reggie joined the line towards the skybridge.

CHAPTER
FORTY-SIX

THEY LANDED in Kinshasa at 6:00 a.m., then took a short flight to Mbandaka, a city up the Congo River, then a boat ride along the Congo River to the Salonga National Park entrance in the Democratic Republic of the Congo. This was the origin of the plant pollen found at the crime scenes, according to Joyce. A golf cart took them down the gravel road and parked outside the reception area. All the structures here had roofs elegantly thatched.

The concierge greeted them and led them to the receptionist, who smiled the way he smiled at tourists. He was dressed in safari khakis and a sun hat with the park's name and logo.

"Welcome. How can I help you today?"

"We have a few questions," Reggie said. She showed her badge.

The receptionist hesitated, showing a little concern. After scrutinizing the I.D., he said, "Should I call the manager?"

"Please do."

He phoned the manager and told her the police

were there. The manager at once came into the room. She looked concerned. She said, "What is not okay? How may I help you?"

"Everything is fine. We only have a few questions. Don't worry, no one is in trouble."

"Please, let's sit in my office."

They followed her to the office.

Once seated, Reggie showed her a picture of the plant on her phone.

"Do you know this plant?"

"It's the Wenge tree. We have these in the park. Why?"

"Did you know that this is the only place on earth where this plant is found?"

"I didn't know that."

"Good. This plant may help solve a homicide."

The manager squirmed in her chair. "In our park?"

"Not in your park. Do you keep a record of your guests?"

"Mainly those who stay in the lodge. But we do have visitors who come for a day's tour. We don't record those."

"What kind of clientele do you get?"

"Everyone. Families, children, young, old. We admit everyone. We have security around the clock, so our premises are safe."

"Do you ever receive people from gangs?"

"Not that I would know of. Thousands of visitors come through here every year," the manager said. "But we also have a problem with poachers. They're usually looking for rare meats and since everything outside the national park is over-hunted, they cut through the fence to get in. There is a huge market for bush meat, and animal parts used in traditional medicine. Most of those guys are associated with syndicates and larger crime rings."

"Where would you look if you wanted to find these crime rings?"

"I don't know. Maybe if you follow the meat trail you will find some answers. I'd start at the Port of Kinshasa meat market."

"Someone was murdered, and the evidence led us here."

"Could be hundreds of people that visit the national park. The poachers maybe are your best bet at finding whoever did this."

"The market at the port of Kinshasa?"

"Go there and ask around. Someone might know. People will give out information if shown the money."

Six and Reggie tipped the manager five dollars and left the reception area to their taxi.

SIX INSERTED the earpiece and listened to his handler while watching the tracker on his phone. He was getting close to where the kidnapped girl's Apple watch was. The directions took him to a market adjacent to the meat market at the Port of Kinshasa. The tracker dot stopped where a group of children were playing in the streets. Six noticed there was only one girl wearing a watch—an Apple watch.

Six approached the children. They were not in the least fazed by his presence. He asked the girl in French where she got the watch. She hid her wrists behind her back.

"My papa got it for me."

"Can you show me where your papa is?"

She nodded. She led him into the market to where her father was facing away from them, sitting and chatting with another man next to a merchant selling bolts of textiles, rugs, and accessories. His daughter gestured to him and then called out, "Papa."

The man turned and looked at his daughter,

then at Six. He rose from the stool and fled, knocking down the rugs, cloths, and several crafts on the next table. He stumbled. Six charged after the man, knocked the man over before he got far, and pinned him to the hard-packed dirt.

"Why did you run?" Six yanked his arm.

The man flinched. "I don't know anything, okay?"

"Where did you get the watch?"

"Take it back."

"I asked you where you got the watch."

"I stole it. I knew that was a bad idea."

"From where?"

"Some people came to the market. I don't know who, okay? This is a city of thousands."

"And you steal from them?"

"Sir, please."

"You know the man you got the watch from?"

"Sir, I don't—"

Six twisted his arm more. "Think."

"I know they were not from around here. They were buying things in bulk. From the Teke tribe based on their accent."

"Are you telling the truth?"

"Yes, sir!"

"I know your family. If I find out that you lied, I know where to find you. Understood?"

"Yes, sir!"

"If you lie to me, I'll find you, and I'll break your fingers one by one."

"Sir, I'm a humble man. I know nothing. Take the watch."

Six stood and let the man go. The man walked back to and embraced his daughter. She cried when asked to hand over the watch. Six decided he had learned all it had to tell him. "Let her keep it," he said.

Six walked toward the meat market. He took a circuitous route through the port area. He always found that revelations about the right course of action always struck him in unexpected areas. The port was a beehive of activities—merchants, fishermen, hunters, shoppers, all congregated, with large, medium, small, and scrappy ferries and boats bringing in the day's catch from the Congo River, and other goods. Farther down was the meat market. It had a stench. There were fish, beef, chicken, and a lot of bush meat: bats, crocodiles, monkeys, antelopes, snakes. Some of the meat was illegal, from animals in danger of extinction. But that's how the locals from villages earned a living to support their families. He passed one or two stands where the vendor was scraping clean the body of a bat, using his teeth.

Six ended up at a small kitchen with several stools and tables. He decided to get something to eat. The setup was simple: You buy the meat, and the cook prepared it for you over the grill. The menu was simple also. Three categories: beef or bush meat, cassava, and vegetables. Today's bush meat selection included snake filet, monkey, tortoise, and antelope.

Six went with the easy choice, ordering a kilogram of beefsteak, and a drink.

"Drink?" said the cook, and motioned to an elderly man tending the braai stand. The old man smiled and nodded at Six.

"Which drink?"

"Water."

The man shrugged. "Only water?"

Six nodded.

Six gave him coins and was handed a bottle of distilled water. Six was reluctant to drink tap water here because of recent cholera outbreaks in the region.

Six then thought to buy a bottle of beer, and brought it to the cook at the grill stand. The man thanked him, sat his cigarette on the grill, and lifted the bottlecap with his teeth. He took a sip and sighed with satisfaction. "Thank you, my friend."

"Everyone seems less friendly here than before," Six said.

"These are troubling times," the cook said, then dragged on his cigarette and blew a cloud of smoke from the right side of his mouth. "And one must tolerate the world as it is."

"Am I missing something?"

"We pay the crime lord every month. If someone doesn't pay, they may die."

"Pay for what?"

"According to them, it's for protection. But the truth is, it's to protect yourself against the same people who claim to protect us. I remember how peaceful things were when I was younger."

"How do you pay them?"

"Tribute—money, grain, meat, and even some send their children to join the leader's forces."

"They give away their children?"

"Or they are taken."

Six waited while the cook salted and seasoned the beef. He laid four fillets on the grill, then stirred the embers from underneath. He then took another gulp of the beer.

"Many girls go missing here," the man said. "No one does anything about it."

"What about the local police?"

"I think some of them are part of the ring. We all know who's taking them."

"Who?"

The man looked at Six. "Are you new here?"

"Yes."

"Keep asking such questions and you will lose your head. No one is going to tell you that name."

"Why doesn't the community investigate all these children disappearing?"

The man shrugged his shoulders. "Me? I only roast meat for customers."

"What else can you tell me?"

"Goats have been disappearing from local farms. The demand for food makes sense. Find where the meat is going and you have your answer."

Five minutes later, the meat was cooked. The man dropped the filets onto a metal plate and handed it to Six. All meat here was cooked the same: well done. Six got a scoop of cassava paste and beans from the lady working in the fire pit and sat on a nearby bench. Cassava, a local staple, was cassava flour, boiled and stirred until thick enough to model by hand into a bolus. The food was good. Six liked it. He shared what he could not finish with people at another table.

BACK AT THE HOTEL, Six found Reggie very angry.

"I was worried," she said. "Tried reaching you and the call kept going to voicemail."

"Sorry. I must have turned the ringer off."

"You can't just go in this naked. You need backup. What if something happens? This region is not very friendly to foreigners right now, especially Americans."

"I know the risks. Sometimes I like doing things my way, alone. It allows me to think straight."

"Please, could you at least give me heads-up next time?"

"I will. I apologize."

Six relayed his findings from the meat market to Reggie, and what he had learned about Colette's watch.

CHAPTER
FORTY-EIGHT

SIX AND REGGIE met Lin at a hotel that afternoon.

"I see you two are still together," Lin said, smiling. She hugged both Reggie and Six.

"I see you haven't lost your wit," Six said.

"What can I say. It's part of me."

"It's good to see you again, old friend," Six said.

"Old friend, huh?"

"It's been a while."

"Both of you look good."

"You too," Reggie said.

"Come this way," Lin said. She led the way to the lounge.

There was a man there apparently waiting for them. He was dressed in traditional attire, all white, and sandals, and a colorful head covering.

"Six, Reggie, this is Isak."

Six and Reggie shook Isak's hand.

"Isak has been my local eyes on the ground for this operation."

"We can't bring guns and artillery into the Republic of the Congo," Isak said. "The borders are tight, especially for foreigners."

"Isak means he will help us smuggle the necessary equipment. He will send us the drop location where we can retrieve the equipment."

Lin spread a map on the coffee table. "From that point, by the national park, we take a canoe three miles up the river to the tavern which is the trailhead to Mubarak's compound."

"You sure this will work?"

"People smuggle stuff in and out. It's a way of life. I trust Isak."

"What if it fails, or he is caught?"

"He is on his own. Isak knows that."

Isak said, "It won't fail. I know the people that move goods through the borders."

"Why not just fly in?" Six said.

"It's closer from this side. Only a fifteen-minute ferry across the river, then an hour's drive from the border between the DRC and Republic of the Congo. Or we could fly into Brazzaville. Then we'd have to drive all the way back down here, which would take several hours. Through a dozen checkpoints."

"The roads in the Republic are worse than here, so it will take longer," Isak said.

"We must go separately," Lin said. "Separate teams and as tourists. A large group will draw eyes."

"I agree. The goal is to get in and out without too much attention."

"This will be tricky. Part of our mission is to free three teenage girls."

"Is there a contingency plan?"

"If things go south," Reggie said. "I will have

my team from AULEB waiting. They can fly in to pick us up. That's a last resort, if necessary. We want to prevent an international conflict."

"I heard no one escapes that compound alive," said Six.

"It is true that no one gets out alive," Isak said. "Only trusted drivers get to leave the compound and sometimes drive all the way here to DRC to buy food and other necessities, basics like tea and sugar. There are shortages in our country after heavy sanctions from the West on the current authoritarian regime. The trucks are heavily armed. Drivers bribe their way through both borders, paying off the ferrymen. I already know the system."

"The goal is, don't get captured," Six said. "If we do we probably won't leave that place."

"The smaller the team, the better," Isak said. "That way the target doesn't get a chance to disappear and take his prisoners with him."

Lin said, "On the same note, we can't carry our own belongings to the other side, so Isak will transport everything we need. We won't be able to cross with anything. The border guards would go crazy."

Six and Reggie nodded.

Reggie observed the map. "What are these buildings?"

Isak said, "Here is the factory where they manufacture illicit drugs."

Lin said, "This one is the mining processing facility and warehouse. Reports say it's used for manufacturing and also for packing large amounts of illicit drugs for export. It was reported that the factory produces several thousand tons of Triple Z,

Meth, and fentanyl alone in addition to trafficking in other drugs, such as heroin. There are extensive hierarchical smuggling and trafficking networks and routes across Africa and Asia. All linked to the compound."

"Updates on Mubarak?"

Lin said, "Mubarak has come to control all the gold, diamonds and lithium mines in the area," Lin said. "Intelligence reports suggest that the gold and diamonds are smuggled to Dubai and the Middle East, while the lithium is sold to China and France."

"Increase in demand for electric cars has produced a lucrative lithium and cobalt market in the region," Isak said.

Lin said, "We also believe Mubarak has an army of assassins that he sends to different parts of the continent. Each one is a private contractor. He gets paid and the job gets done."

"So all these attacks may be linked to him," Six said.

"Yes," Lin said. "A distraction from his illegal money-making machine."

"We are close to having enough evidence to prosecute him," Lin continued. "As I said, every dictator eventually makes a mistake. And that one mistake is what our team needs to break through."

"I doubt Mubarak runs everything," Reggie said. "The guys in the bush are never on top, and the guy on top is never in the trenches. The one calling all the financial shots, laundering the money, has to be elsewhere. We have to get information out of Mubarak if we can."

Isak checked his wristwatch. "I have to go before my colleagues find I'm not in my room," Isak said.

"Thank you, Isak," Lin said.

Isak put his headdress on and vanished into the night.

"You trust him?" Reggie said.

"Yes. Mubarak acquired several thousand hectares by supplanting the locals. One of the former owners offered to guide us to the spot where they killed Isak's parents in the process. Isak was seven years old then."

CHAPTER
FORTY-NINE

EARLY THE NEXT MORNING, Six and Reggie woke up in Kinshasa, freshened up, put on their khakis and jeans, packed their backpacks, and looked just like tourists. The ferry port was a few kilometers from their hotel. They arrived at the ferry port before 6:00 a.m. to beat the crowds. The taxi dropped them at the gate that led to customs. There they converted their money to the local currency at a stall with a handwritten sign that read "Forex Exchange" both in French and in English.

The whole border-crossing process was disorderly and involved bribes. Isak had paired Six and Reggie with a fixer, a guy whom they paid a sizable amount to have all their border checks done efficiently and without too many questions. The fixer was waiting for them at the ferry point. His fee included bribing some of the port officials. He took their passports, entered a small office, then a few minutes later returned with the passports and their ferry tickets. They showed their passports to the four policemen sitting at the gate, then completed the immigration forms and cleared customs.

The fixer handed cash to the immigration officer who stamped passports. Another officer took their passports again, and asked for their reason for visit. They would be in Brazzaville for a week, as tourists, they said. Several minutes later, he called their names and directed them down the ferry entrance.

Once they were in the ferry, they were handed very old life vests and assigned seats. The boat departed shortly. Fourteen minutes later they were on the Republic of the Congo side, at the Congo-Brazzaville port. Clearing customs on the Republic of the Congo side was challenging and frustrating with long waits, countless questions, and paying bribes to the officials and officers. Everything was still analogue, done with papers, handwriting, and rubber stamps. The officials tried to squeeze more money from them. Six was annoyed. Under normal circumstances he would have refused, but he knew time was not on their side. They passed through five security checks, guards inspecting their visas and backpacks, and at every point asking questions. At every checkpoint they were asked to pay two- or three-dollar bribes. A five-dollar bribe let you skip the line. They finally received their stamped passports and exited the office and caught a taxi: an old Toyota Avion.

They asked the taxi driver where they could get rides to the village.

"Sir, very few cars go that direction," the driver said.

"Why not?" Six said.

"The roads are bad. So bad."

"How can we get there?"

"I know people who go there. I can show you."

He looked at them in the back seat, via his rear-view mirror.

"Take us to them."

"But you must pay. They want money." He emphasized his point rubbing his thumb against his index finger.

"How much?"

"A thousand francs. Congolese francs."

"Take us to this place."

The driver navigated past heaps of trash as the street cleaners were busy cleaning trash from the previous day. He reached an open space outside a supermarket where several UD trucks were parked. He rolled down the windows and told Six and Reggie to wait while he went and talked to one of the drivers. He came back later smiling.

"Sir, this one agreed. He is passing close to that area."

"Good. Let's go."

"But fifteen hundred francs, sir."

"You said one thousand."

"I did. But the roads are no good. He said it will damage his truck."

"Twelve hundred."

The driver shook his head. "He will not. I tried."

"Okay. When is he leaving?"

The taxi driver looked at his Seiko watch. "In five minutes, sir."

Six handed the man fifteen hundred francs. The man took the money and stood.

"For me, sir, one hundred francs only, for a drink."

Six sighed and handed the man a hundred francs.

"Thank you very much, sir. Follow me."

They boarded the truck that delivered groceries to the area on the eastern edge of the city, past the lines of old warehouses. There were several others, women and children, in the open truck bed. They sat on top of bags of maize and other wholesale products. The driver told them the journey was only twenty-five miles. They also learned the driver traveled with three helpers and a mechanic —the former to fend off robbers, and the latter to fix the truck on anticipated breakdowns, which happened often on these roads. They stopped by an old convenience store, and bought several accessories for the journey, whatever they could find. No basic items. One extra liter of fuel.

From Brazzaville, they drove north. The tarmac turned to gravel, which became worse and worse as they drove farther from the city. The driver slowly navigated roads muddy and treacherous from torrential rains and floods, which were frequent. A road made only of mud meandered through the jungle. They passed a few broken-down vehicles and beat-up delivery trucks, motorcycles, and overloaded minibuses that were spinning their wheels in the mud. Their own truck got stuck in the mud. Locals, for a reasonable price, helped to push and pull their vehicle using ropes pulled by oxen and men, women, and children, while others laid tree logs in the muddy trench in front of the car for the wheels to grip so the truck could move forward. Above all, the local people smiled, happy despite their condition.

After they were unstuck they drove for about two miles. Then there was sound from bearings grinding, until the wheels couldn't move. The mechanic checked the wheels. The ball bearings had fallen off. Everyone got out of the truck, helped unload it and jack it up. The mechanic then carved new ball bearings out of wood. After two hours they reloaded the truck and were back on the road again. Surprisingly, the wooden bearings were strong enough to cover the remaining kilometers without any issues or catching fire.

Ten hours later, they reached the village. The journey of twenty-five miles had taken ten hours. Six and Reggie's backs were stiff from the jolting and twisting as the truck maneuvered the un-graded road.

CHAPTER
FIFTY

THE TEAM MET at a motel at a small growth point west of the village north of Brazzaville.

Lin, Isak, and the four men and two women from Reggie's team from the Bureau's special forces were already there when Six and Reggie got to the growth point.

After a break for introductions, Lin shared the maps and satellite images. Earlier in the day, the team had deployed two reconnaissance drones into the forest for a close-up aerial surveillance of the terrain.

"The arms needed to approach to Mubarak's compound will be best transported by water," said Lin, indicating the river that bordered on Mubarak's compound. "Mubarak of course stays in the chateau at the center of the compound, slightly elevated above every other structure. Usually, it's guarded by at least ten or twenty armed men with AK-47s. The rest of the housing is for his soldiers and his wives. No wives, though. We think Mubarak thought they knew too much."

"How many people are we expecting?"

"A hundred at least, fighting men."

"We will need more firepower to get through."

"I can help with that," Reggie said. "They can all be brought upriver before tonight and stashed in the woods near the outer perimeter."

Six said, "That's going to be almost impossible to evade the search floodlight."

"No moon tonight," Lin said. "Expecting heavy clouds. Should give us cover from the tower guards. If we stay close to the trees away from the search light, we can make it to the gate."

"And the girls?"

Isak spoke. "We must pass the second row of buildings all the way to the rear. There is an underground prison behind the training grounds. Most likely they are there."

Six said, "The best approach would be to divide into three teams, A, B and C. One team will go straight to the rear of the compound closest to the place where we think the hostages are. One on the flank, closest to where Mubarak should be, and the compound's garage. Another one to the front to keep the guards occupied. Remember we expect heavy fire, so the stealthier and swifter we are the better. Let's take as many of them as possible quietly. I know being fired upon is inevitable."

Six continued, "Reggie, your and team's mission is to secure the hostages."

Isak said, "Most of the guards are at the front and around the main house."

"Good. Lin and I will take Teams A and B. Our goal is to distract the guards. Team C, Reggie's team, frees the girls, and Team B gets to Mubarak."

"The wall is fortified with an electric fence," Lin

said, "and a front tower. The big metal gate has usually eight to ten guards."

"I will get in and find the key or the key code," Six said.

Isak raised his brows.

"I can go first," Lin said. "I'm small. They won't see me."

"You don't know that."

"Then I will go with you."

"Fine," Six said. "Reggie and the rest, you advance after we are in. Lin, wait for me this time before you start killing. I know you want to have all the fun."

Lin smiled. "I'll try, but can't promise you. You know how I operate. I do things fast."

"How do we turn off the electric fence?"

"Their main switch is in the shop close to the garage," Isak said.

"Can you get to it? Can you operate it?"

Isak hesitated.

"Then you will be with Lin and me," said Six. "Your job is to turn that electricity off."

"I can."

"Good," Six said. "We will need that electric fence and lights off to get the children out. We will armor up, wait, coordinate, and try to do this in thirty minutes. In and out, like were never there."

Isak said, "We only have a thirty-minute window after we disable the nearby telecommunications tower. The off-grid electricity will then restart the electricity and communications within the compound. Someone will radio for help, and we must be out of there before backup arrives."

"We intercepted a communication from that camp," Lin told Six. "They are expecting two trucks in, with what they said was important cargo."

"They should be sulphur trucks," Isak said. "There is a sulphur mine just down the river, and the trucks return at day's end."

"Are you sure it's sulphur?"

"They use it to make bombs."

"But we don't know the precise time they are coming in."

"I drive one of those trucks, and the best plan would be to enter when our trucks clock out of the gates at the sulphur mine," Isak said. "At days' end all the trucks leave the mines, drive to their respective factories, get receipts, then head back to the garage along this route, and meet and travel like a caravan. That way the guards open the gate only once and can be sure that all truckers from all mines have returned and been accounted for."

"When does the sulphur mine clock out?"

"All the mine workers clock out at 6:00. The last of the minerals and ore get driven to their pro-cessing factories. Then the drive to join the caravan usually takes us forty-five minutes to an hour. Then they all head to the compound, getting there between 8:00 and 8:30. I will make sure my truck is the last one. You can trail behind. I know the guards, and usually they let us in without check-ing. But it depends on who is on duty."

"Perfect. Lin and I will tag under your truck and use this to get into the camp, past the guards. Will you or will you not be able to convince the guard not to search the truck?"

"I can't say. It depends on who is on duty. I will try."

"Works for me," Six said.

"So, we tag on the truck. Then what?" said Lin.

"Once you're past the gates, it's all you," Isak said. "That's all I can do."

"We can take it from there," Six said. "How much firepower are we expecting?"

"A lot," Isak said. "There are guards at every post. In the compound, possibly close to a hundred on night patrol. But if the siren goes off, more will come."

"We can take them out."

"We will need to disable the communication in and out of the compound, one hundred percent. That can be done. The receivers and boosters are all located in the garage area. It is a box with switches they think cannot be hacked like digital."

"Can you get to it?"

"Yes."

"Isak then will wait for us in the garage, cut the power and destroy every other vehicle," Lin said. "Then we will bring the hostages to this point here, and he drives us out."

"Yes, they keep only vehicles that can move out of there using the route we are taking. We then drive overland to the river and cross the border into DRC before midnight. Men will smuggle us across the river away from the border officials. So the return trip shouldn't be a problem."

"You have done this before."

"Many times. People are fleeing south to the DRC for work and livelihood. The smugglers give a cut to the police, so the police leave them alone."

Everyone nodded.

"Once on the DRC side we will have trucks waiting for us. Then a forty-minute drive to a private airstrip. We should be in the air by 1:00 a.m."

"I like the plan."

"About the hostages?" Reggie said.

"The hostages will be delivered here." Lin pointed to the satellite image.

"How many guys are on the rescue team?" Six said.

"I have requested six more of our squad of elites from the bureau," Reggie said. "They are women. The male guards will for a split-second underestimate them, giving the team a split-second more of an advantage. That is all that is needed. They will move the hostages to safety."

"Me and my guys will move through here to get to Mubarak as fast as possible before an alarm is raised," said Six. "Reggie, your people take the rear, extract the hostages, get them in the truck. Lin, do what you do best. Go with Isak and get to the generators and transformers as fast as you can to permanently disable all power and telecommunications. Clear the path for Isak for when he is ready to roll. Everyone got that?"

Six had another thought. He turned to Isak and said, "How will you be able to get out with hostages under a rain of bullets? Your tipper won't withstand their bullets."

"There are two old German military trucks in the garage. I will have to get the keys to one from the guy who guards the garage. That will be the safest vehicle to make it out alive."

"Crunch time," Reggie said.

"I must go," Isak said. "I have to be at work soon."

Six said, "Let's all be on top of our game to get the girls home safely. And kill Mubarak. And then we are out."

CHAPTER
FIFTY-ONE

THE AFTERNOON GREW chilly and formed mist. The team waited until sunset, and the leaders of each team took a gondola five kilometers up the river, and the gondolier let them off at a fishing village on the riverbank. Lin had brought body armor in a duffle bag. They had each chosen a firearm and brought several extra magazines. Six chose an AK-47 and packed several magazines in his vest and belt. He also chose two SIG pistols, which he strapped to his thigh and his waist. He added eight remote-controlled bombs to his vest. Last, he strapped his wooden club across his back and put a pair of night-vision optics on his head. Reggie and Lin had done the same.

The fog and drizzle were clearing when they reached the fishing village. Two remote-controlled lightweight unmanned ground vehicles led the way ahead of the team to clear any mines. The mine-clearing robots detected three mines in their path which the crew deactivated remotely. The team walked north from the village deep into the forest before separating. They reached their waiting spots where they found their reinforcements ready with extra weaponry. They waited.

Streaks of light appeared in the forest from a distance. Then the sound of diesel trucks followed. One of Reggie's team members confirmed the number of trucks approaching using visuals from the two robot vehicles sent down the road. The last three tipper trucks arrived at exactly 8:00 p.m.

Six and Lin vanished into the dark. They tailed the last truck on either side, keeping out of its rear-view mirror for about a quarter mile. When nearing the compound's perimeter they waited a few yards before climbing and strapping themselves flat beneath the truck bed. At the open gate, each of the trucks was searched by soldiers and by hounds. The last truck stopped at the metal gate where two guards searched around it and inside of the truck bed with flashlights. Their security hounds sniffed around. The loads of sulphur-scented sunscreen on Six and Lin masked their scents and the dogs did not detect them, and ran back to the guard house wagging their tails. The guard said something to the driver, then the truck moved forward.

Six and Lin rolled from under the truck onto the lawn and sprinted up the green pathway, using the hedge as cover. From a short distance Six and Lin killed all the guardhouse guards and their two hounds. Six and Lin dashed across the lawn and dove behind the hedge. Two guards passed. Six attached a silencer onto his SIG pistol and nodded "yes" to Lin.

Reggie's team now had an open path to their target. They were green figures in Six and Lin's night optics. Six and Lin swept the area with their silenced guns. They fired several rounds, each claiming a victim. Three more green figures appeared on their night optics. Three quick shots, and they were down, the sound of their falling dampened by the wet lawn. They advanced to the courtyard and working together attached several timed bombs to the fuel tank and cars around the chateau.

The team moved in shortly. After all teams were through the gate, they approached the compound in a three-pronged attack. The triad advanced in a V-shape, Six's team blazing the front, while Reggie and Lin's teams covered the flanks. Near the chateau they separated, each group to its assignment.

Six rolled beneath a G-wagon at the front of the mansion, dashed past the water fountain and crouched as two guards passed by; his companions nearby would eliminate them. Then he tiptoed towards the arched stairs using a line of potted shrubs as a shield. He shot the one guard at the top of the stairs, looked back to check that his team was making progress, then gently pushed open the large teakwood front doors. He was in.

There was no one in the foyer. Six dashed across the marble floor and hid beneath the stairs. He heard two voices approaching. He caught the two men by surprise, crushing each man's skull with a single blow of his club the instant before they could react and reach for their AK-47s. He pulled the bodies under the staircase and checked his watch. Isak and Lin ought to be at the power source now. He waited. A few seconds later the lights flickered and died. He could hear increasingly urgent voices from the courtyard as several guards rushed toward the power station and the transformers, forgetting to start the chateau's generator.

Six tiptoed up the spiral staircase. From Isak he knew where Mubarak's master bedroom was. Of course, it was at the highest point in the chateau and therefore the highest point in the compound, overlooking it all. A stupidly predictable place. Two more guards shuffled past him as Six stayed in the shadows.

MUBARAK WOKE up in a cold sweat. He had had a bad dream. He blinked, adjusting to the darkness. He wiped sleep from his eyes and looked towards the window, seeing only darkness with flashes of light and hearing AK-47s. A commotion had erupted. He reached for the lamp switch on the nightstand. It wasn't working. He hit a bedside button to summon his guards. No response. That's when he noticed a silhouette sitting on the accent chair at the foot of his bed. Mubarak reached for the 9mm on his nightstand. With both hands he pulled the trigger. The gun clicked, but did not fire. In a frenzy, he pulled the trigger ten more times, each time frustrated, until the 9mm was hopelessly jammed.

"Old man," the man in the shadows said. "The magazine is empty." He dropped the ten bullets he was holding in his hand onto the bed, one by one.

"Who are you?" Mubarak said straining his eyes. It was too dark to see the intruder's face.

"Does it matter? Today is your last day to live."

"You're bluffing."

Six did not answer.

"How did you get in here? What do you want?"

Six checked his watch.

Mubarak felt some stiffness in his arm and let go of the useless empty pistol.

"What have you done to me?"

"It's tetrodotoxin from a puffer fish," Six said. "I injected a dose enough to paralyze every muscle, but you remain conscious and feel the pain. Of dying."

"What, what have—? Guards! Guards!"

"I would say 'burn in hell,' but that would be too easy for you. I want you to see your empire burn to ashes while you burn right here, and you can't do anything about it," Six said. "I want you to feel the pain of all the families—fathers, moms, children, you tortured and killed, and forced to work for you and do your bidding."

"You think I'm afraid of dying? I have died many times! I have survived assassins just like you!"

"I'm not those other people."

"I survived. I was chosen to do this. This is my purpose. My destiny. To rule."

Six did not answer.

Mubarak's whole arm began to stiffen and he was frightened.

Six checked his watch again. Mubarak said, his voice pleading, "Who are you? What have you done to me?"

"I will spare you the gory details. You're going to die. Right here. With all your gold and Chinese silk and Egyptian cotton. A slow, painful death. Alright, time for the show." Six stood, then opened the heavy curtains opposite the bed so Mubarak could see most of his compound. It was dark with flashes of gunfire. Mubarak sat, his eyes wide open no matter how hard he tried to close them.

Six placed a bomb on the bed. *Fifteen minutes.*

Mubarak struggled for words. "Our people will keep coming and new people will take over."

"Let them. I will be waiting for them!"

Six left the room.

CHAPTER
FIFTY-TWO

SIX LEFT Mubarak shell-shocked and helpless. He stepped out of the master bedroom and down a set of stairs onto the mezzanine. An axe missed his head by inches and planted itself into the wooden doorframe.

"Shit!" Six ducked and slid across the tiled floor while unloading more bullets in the direction the axe had come from. He got one of the men. Four more, throwing knives, missed him narrowly as he rolled away. Six saw he was trapped. Knife-wielding ninjas blocked the way down to the ground floor. Six looked down between the banisters at the foyer, deliberating whether to jump. He had two choices: Either he jumped, or he went through the knife-wielders. The jump would likely mess up his knees permanently. He chose the latter. First, Six ripped a painted portrait of Napoleon Bonaparte from the wall. He hurled the painting at the three men. Then a flying kick collided with a man who was running full blast at him, machete in hand. Six finished him off with a bullet to the forehead. More bullets rang. Six used the man as a shield and emptied his pistol in the direction the bullets were coming from. Several men fell over the mezzanine. The exit to the staircase was now blocked by two men with knives and monkey hats.

Six aimed and pulled the trigger. His gun clicked—several times. Empty magazine. He felt for a magazine on his bulletproof vest and thigh strap. None. *Crap!* He thought he might see Lin, but she and Isak were doing their jobs. He debated whether to take the assault rifle from his latest victim. He chose not to. It was too loud. Six unstrapped the club from his back and advanced. He thought that would do.

He picked up the framed painting and used it as a shield. The first man came swinging the machete, slashing. Six parried his moves by trapping the blade into the canvas, spinning around, and twisting it. The assailant let go of the weapon. They squared off again. The man plunged into Six with a flying kick. The kick caught Six on the side of his head, crushing his earpiece. He staggered backwards, then shook it off, just in time, as the man pressed forward with a high roundhouse kick. Six ducked and planted his left heel into the man's groin. The man groaned. Six followed this with a double thrust with such force the man toppled over the mezzanine railing and thudded on the floor below.

The last man charged, raining down a combination of kicks, jabs, clawing, blade arches, and hoarse-voiced hollering. All in the air. It was a beauty. Six waited. With one move, Six struck the man on the temple with the club. He dropped. Six rushed down the staircase.

Another man came flying up the staircase

swinging a metal rod. The metal rod smashed into Six's wrist, cracking his watch's crystal. *Dang it!* The wrist was painful, but he sensed it was not broken. Six chopped him with a low roundhouse kick. The man flipped, his head crashing on the gilded stair railings with such force that his skull chipped off the wood and gilding.

Meanwhile, Lin's team and Isak had blazed their way to the garage. There were many cars, divided into trucks, vans, and personal cars, from the cheapest old Defender to several Mercedes G-wagons and two Rolls Royces. Lin guessed the collection was worth tens of millions of dollars. A gun cracked. One of Lin's crew, who were disabling all of the cars' batteries, dropped dead. Both Lin and Isak dove for cover.

"Shit! Man down!" Lin said. She fired in the direction of the bullets and then took cover behind a pile of bricks.

Lin then shot the garage's guard. They reached the office, which led into the main control room. Isak disabled the electric fence and lights and attached a bomb to what looked like the electrical power master control so no one would dare to touch it. In the office Isak fiddled with a bunch of key fobs and car keys in a drawer and then selected one. He led Lin past a line of dump trucks to a green and black camouflaged Herman MAN Category 1 Heavy High Mobility Truck. The German army had used these eight-by-eight military trucks in the 1970s and 1980s. This one was dented and pitted, and left unfixed; the flaws were like marks of honor.

"Out the gate!" Lin radioed to her team. "Out, out! Now!" They knocked about in the garage's darkness, then fled outside and through the gate. Then she said to Isak, "You know how to drive this thing?"

"Let's go," Isak said.

"Reggie!" Lin said, as the engine roared to life. "Team C, can you hear me? Update on hostages!"

"In sight. Under heavy fire!"

"Let's go!" Isak said. "And brace yourself."

Isak rammed the truck into the garage wall. The wall collapsed. The truck blasted through and leveled the brick wall around the courtyard, and rolled the right over the hedgerows, then knocked down the water fountain with its lion sculpture. It nicked the parked G-wagon at the front of the big chateau, then swerved left toward the rear of the property where the holding cells were.

CHAPTER
FIFTY-THREE

REGGIE'S TEAM made their way to the holding cells. They killed more guards. Bullets rained and ricocheted as she and her team neared the holding cells. Reggie fired back, taking out two guards defending the holding cells.

Reggie saw that the gate and the cells had traditional key locks. A team member ran to the downed guards and frisked them for keys. She retrieved a ring of keys and they were in.

"Colette!" Reggie called down the long halls of holding cells to the left and right of the gate. Reggie's voice echoed. There was no answer. She gestured with her flashlight. "Go that way," she said to her team, "and I'll go this way."

After finishing Mubarak and getting down the stairs, Six still had to fight his way out because more and more guards appeared, armed with AK47s. Six kept killing, blood all over his face and arms, and when he got out the door he ran blindly into the darkness, out of breath.

The guards up in the watchtower were on alert and armed with machine guns. Six's night-vision optics showed him there were two guards, and without their searchlight they had to fire blindly, so they simply kept firing. Six was in the line of fire. One bullet caught him on his bulletproof vest, on the chest. It hurt like hell. Six clenched his teeth against the pain. But the bullet let Six know the watchtower was in front of him, and to reach the rear of the property he'd have to double back, fast; the teams had only thirty minutes, and he'd wasted precious time savoring Mubarak's death and then fighting Mubarak's thugs. The farther he got from the watchtower the less accurate the guards' firepower would be. The gate into the holding cells was already open when he got there.

All the holding cells were empty. Reggie's team had found sets of stairs on each end leading underground to a concrete-walled hall, pitch-dark. The team's flashlights showed the faces of twenty terrified factory kids from the dorm bunched up in the dark, trying to cling to the three teenagers, all of them hearing the gunfire and screams above ground. The place stank.

"We're the law! You're okay!" said Reggie. "Form two lines!" Reggie briefly stepped close to the teenagers and said, "You must fight." With flashlights, her team herded the kids, the teenagers first, into two lines and motioned each line toward the stairs on each end of the room. As Colette's group was mounting their staircase, a guard with a battery-powered headlamp charged down the stairs. Colette knocked him into the concrete wall. In a flash, Colette jumped onto the guard's back, wrapping her hands around his throat.

"Leave us alone!" she said.

She plunged the sharpened spoon handle into

the man's soft tissue between the collarbone and neck. The man screamed and shrugged the girl off. With one hand he shoved and pinned her shoulder against the wall, and with his other hand circled her neck and pressed his thumb on her throat. "You'll pay, little bitch!" he said.

Then sounded a crack of hard wood on skull bone. Blood sprayed from the man's temple. The guard's grip on Colette loosened. He looked shell-shocked, let her go, and sank to his knees. Colette held her neck, gasping. Six disarmed the guard and said to Colette, "You are safe now. Your father sent us."

"Go! Go! Go!" Six shouted. "Let's move! We have seven minutes!"

"This way," Reggie said. "Follow my lead."

Reggie's team carried some of the malnour-ished children. They filed towards the exit. Six was last to leave. With his club Six bashed the guard's head and headlamp in, and he had his 9mm pistol.

Six then ran to take his place in front of the line of children, with Reggie's rescue team flanking them and Reggie covering the rear.

CHAPTER
FIFTY-FOUR

SIX AND REGGIE led the children out of the holding facility towards a truck that barreled toward them and then came screeching to a halt. They loaded the children into the back of the truck as quickly as possible.

"Let's move," Reggie said.

Then came more gunshots from behind them. One of Reggie's team members went down.

Six told Reggie, "Go! I'll hold them off."

"I'm staying with you."

"The kids! Get them to safety. Don't stop until you reach the extraction point."

The truck's rear door slammed shut. Lin was yelling, "Isak, step on it!" Isak threw the truck into gear as more gunfire spattered around it, and sped toward the front gate, which was now unguarded and gaping. More gunfire rang. Shrapnel ricocheted from AK-47 fire that hit the brick wall.

Six aimed at the direction of the gunfire and fired the 9mm. A guard fell. *The more I kill, the more keep coming,* he thought, and he was dismayed to see fog now forming at ground level; the earth was warm and the air was cold.

"Where's Six?" Lin said.

"He said we should not wait."

Bullets cracked against the truck's windshield, interrupting their talk.

"Lie down, kids!"

Reggie's team got all the children to lie flat. There were bumps as the truck ran over scattered bodies.

From the tower a greenish figure launched an EFP.

"Incoming!" Lin said. Isak swerved just enough for the projectile to miss and blew up a few meters to the side of the truck. The explosion caused the truck to tilt. Then it rebalanced itself.

"I'll get him," Lin said.

Lin climbed to the roof hatch where a machine gun was mounted, aimed, fired, and the guard toppled from the tower.

Several of Mubarak's guards had mobilized and blocked the gate using two old Humvees. The truck's armored rigid chassis and tires were able to withstand the showers of bullets from every direction, but the front windshield finally cracked. Lin, still on the roof hatch, sprayed bullets towards the barricade.

"The truck is not bulletproof!" Isak said. He saw nothing to do but smash through the two Humvees blocking the exit, crushing the guards who were using them as perches and shields.

The truck burst through the gate and sped on.

WITH THE HELP OF A GUIDE, at a wide point in the Congo River, all of the children, plus Lin and the four surviving members of Reggie's team, were loaded onto an old rusty barge that had been made to operate silently with pedals. They were then pedaled across the river, in the fog and against the current, by the light of a single paraffin lamp. On the other side of the river, the teenagers and children were swiftly loaded into two UD trucks headed to the extraction point, a private airstrip.

Reggie waited on the riverbank and Isak on the dock until the transporters brought the barge back. Lin stayed with the children on the other side of the river. After twenty minutes Isak came to Reggie and spoke.

"We should leave," he said. "Some of the transporters are getting restless."

"We'll wait a little bit longer."

Reggie paced back and forth.

"If he doesn't come back—" Isak said.

"I know he will be here!"

Isak stayed silent and left Reggie and joined the transporters at the barge.

A few minutes later their guide, who was standing watch at a distance, came running.

The guide gasped, "A truck is approaching!"

The transporters turned out the paraffin lantern and waited. Faint headlights came into view. Reggie had her gun aimed and ready. A Humvee plowed through the riverside mud to a halt. Then its driver's side door creaked open, and a figure emerged out of the fog.

"It's Six," Reggie said, already halfway running to him.

Isak and Reggie helped Six onto the barge. His body was covered in tar and ashes. He smelled of gasoline. Parts of his battle gear had been burnt off. He was shaking.

"Bring water. He needs water!" Reggie said.

As the barge began moving, Six held Reggie's hand. He said, "I thought you already left."

"Not without you."

"Is Colette okay?"

"All the children are safe."

"Thank God!"

Six passed out.

BY MIDNIGHT they were back near Kinshasa at the extraction point. The children had been placed into several tents that Reggie's AULEB team had erected. They were fed, cleaned up, and the sick children, and then Six, received medical treatment. Six, Reggie, and Lin slept in the staff tent. Isak stayed in a separate hotel in town.

Chris's private plane arrived at the airstrip at dawn and the family chauffeur promptly drove up, in a Jeep.

Six, Lin, and Reggie waited by the airstrip. After some sleep, Six was feeling better. Lin hugged both Six and Reggie.

"You two take care of each other, okay?" she said.

Six said to Lin, "Why do I have a feeling we will run into each again?"

"Serendipity. Maybe we are meant to work together?"

"Take care of yourself," Six said.

"Where to now?" Lin said.

"I don't know. See more of the world. Hike. Eat."

"You can't beat that."

She hugged Reggie again. "You take care of yourself."

"What will you do about the Mubarak bank accounts?" Reggie said to Lin.

"As soon as I am sure I have the records I will give it back to the rightful owners, and those we can prove were knowingly financing human and drug trafficking will be tried in court. They will have to forfeit their portion and it will be a good start if we set up a fund for the kids and their families. All of it will go to them—maybe help with schooling, food, and much needed support. Build better roads, clinics, and so on."

"That's nice," Reggie said. "My people are working on finding the children's relatives. If they cannot be found, we can arrange proper homes for the children."

"Definitely don't send the money to the FBI or MI6," said Six. "If it goes there, none of it will ever come back to help the people here."

"Agreed," Lin said, and then a car arrived for her, and she left.

Chris and Sheila's Jeep pulled up. Colette was in it, having said goodbye to Judith and Priscilla at the tent where the girls had spent the night. Colette hopped out, ran up to them and hugged Reggie.

"Detective Kona, thank you for saving me and my friends. I want to be just like you," Colette told her. "A detective who does what you do."

"Ahem," said Chris, who had other plans for his daughter.

"You fought bravely," Reggie said to Colette. She turned to Chris and Sheila and said, "Your daughter has the gift of leadership. When we got to her, Colette had managed to free most of the children."

Both parents smiled proudly.

Then Colette hugged Six. She lingered, then gave him a peck on the cheek.

"Thank you, Six," she said.

"I'm glad you're okay."

"I mean it. Thank you so much."

Six smiled.

"Let me know next time you are in Cape Town," said Colette.

"You bet."

Sheila said, "Okay. Leave Mr. Six alone. It's time to go home."

Then Sheila said, "I can't thank you enough for bringing my daughter back. You should visit us in Cape Town sometime soon. The orphanage ribbon-cutting is in a month."

"Thank you, Mrs. Osage. We will see."

"You two take care of yourself," Chris said. "You both could use some rest and a good meal. And thank you again for bringing our baby back. I will see you tomorrow before we leave."

"You're welcome," Reggie said.

Colette waved as the vehicle drove off.

"See," said Reggie, "Looks like you got yourself another admirer. Told you, you are good with the ladies."

Six laughed. "I'm just happy the kid is safe."

"But still?"

Six smirked. "I think they have a term for that—?"

"Knight in shining armor!"

Six said, "The kid met you yesterday and today you are her idol! I'm thankful that her parents have the resources to make sure she gets the therapy she is going to need."

CHAPTER
FIFTY-SIX

THE AU HEADQUARTERS building in Addis Ababa was combed for bugs ahead of Africa Day and the delegates' meeting, and none were found, debunking conspiracy theories that the Chinese contractors who had renovated the building had installed sophisticated listening devices for espionage. If Six and his team did not find any, there were definitely none there.

Security teams from the AU Intelligence and Law Enforcement Bureau offices were already at the AU headquarters, on alert. Several armed guards were stationed at the entrance. Twenty more officers and security dogs patrolled the perimeter of the building and several more were stationed at different checkpoints within the building. Press points had been set up in the meeting hall where credentialed reporters from the international media would broadcast the voting results, live, after the deliberation was complete.

Six and Reggie passed the security check at the entrance where they handed off their handguns, then walked through two metal detectors, and then their handguns were returned to them. They went downstairs to the monitoring room. Technicians were monitoring every security camera at every possible entrance, and all the hallways inside the building.

The motorcade transporting the document had arrived at the AU headquarters that morning. Carried inside, the document was securely locked in a vault in the west wing of the building, a steel-reinforced, super-hardened section of the building designed to withstand a thousand pounds of blast pressure and heat from a direct missile attack. Several other motorcades arrived, bringing all fifty-four delegates from each of the member states, escorted by soldiers and the local police. Much to everyone's surprise, the chairman of the Assembly, Mr. Mussa, arrived last, wearing traditional Tanzanian attire, and in a wheelchair. Most thought he was dead. He wheeled himself through the doorway and hallways, halted and posed for photographers at the door of the African Union's F. Mussa Law Library, and eventually allowed himself to be grandly wheeled by soldiers in full dress to the front of the voting chamber.

Mussa called the meeting to order, and after a traditional welcome to all, proceeded to give his opening speech. After that, deliberations would commence.

An officer in the monitoring room said to Six, "Sir, we have intercepted a phone call for you."

Six nodded, nudged Reggie, and pressed his cellphone's answer key.

Six signaled the officer to record and trace the call.

"Who's this?" Six said.

The coarse French accent on the other end spoke. "This is not over," the voice said, then coughed. Six could hear the man blowing cigar smoke. "I'm just getting started."

"Who is this?"

"We are going to show the world. You think these little theatricals you are putting on will change our course. No." The speaker gave a quiet laugh.

"State your business."

"You know what I want."

"Whatever you are, we do not intend to fulfill your needs."

"You are twisting my arm here, Agent Six. What happens next is all on you."

"We do not respond to terrorist threats, whether you like it or not."

"I admire your courage. But like I said, what happens next is on you."

The call ended.

The guards and technicians in the room were looking at Six, concerned.

The officer had not been able to trace the call. "Possibly he could be using makeshift devices or an Internet call. VPN makes it difficult to locate where he might be. Could be anywhere in the world. Even in this building."

"Did you hear the background echoes?" said Six. "I think he is in the building and close to the chamber, maybe calling from a lavatory. Everyone, search for a man with glasses, possibly with a false mustache. And check every CCTV for any suspicious faces."

"He smokes," said Reggie. "If he is in the building you'll be able to sniff him out."

"What a fool," said Six. "He must want to be found. Rewind the footage from the last fifteen minutes."

Extra guards gathered in the monitoring room and received their orders.

With the chief technician, Six and Reggie reviewed the front door's CCTV footage at twice the normal speed.

"Rewind that," Six said. "Pause there!" Six approached the screen and pointed. "I've seen this guy before."

There was the man in glasses carrying a briefcase. He was issued a lanyard and passed through the front security checkpoint with ease.

"Fake credentials!" said Six. "Where'd he get them?"

"Here, watch the hallway in the eastern wing, camera facing west," said a technician. The video showed the man on his way past the law library toward the voting chamber.

"I've seen that face before in Tangier. And the same walk," Six said.

The tech zoomed into the man's I.D. badge.

"What's his nametag say?"

"He is one of the personal guards for the Congolese delegate."

"Then why isn't he with him? Is he on the list? Check the directory. You must have the names of all the people here. We know he speaks French. What name did he give?"

The technician said, "Any name would be a false or misleading name. Bodyguards at the delegates' level never give out their real names. More accurate, we should try to match the photo on his credentials." After a minute he said, "I can't seem to find a photo that matches. Here are some that come close."

"Dammit! He is our guy. Can you run facial recognition?"

"Yes, sir. That will take a while. It is through an online app."

Six became angry. "You don't have facial recognition?"

"Our software is out of order, sir."

Most of the monitors showed the meeting room and the delegates, or Mussa as he addressed them about the importance of the vote that was soon to be taken. Minutes ticked by.

"Sir, the database query didn't bring any hits."

Six paced back and forth. "How did he get in here?"

"Possibly there are several people working with him inside the building," Reggie said.

Six and Reggie locked eyes.

"You're thinking of Ophélie?" Reggie said.

"I am thinking of Ophélie. Damn her."

"But how?"

"I will explain later."

A technician from the rear of the room spoke up. "Among the attendees are four with French passports. Two are members of the press."

"Where did they station the personal guards?"

"In the auditorium next to the voting chamber, sir."

"They have direct access to the chamber?"

"Yes, sir."

"Let's move! Lock all the entrances and exits. No one goes in or out. Guards, prepare to evacuate everyone to the bunker in case there is a bomb. And do it quietly! We don't want panic."

Six phoned his contact number for Ophélie. She didn't answer.

Six and Reggie sprinted up the stairs.

"How do we disarm a bomb if we find it? We don't have an expert on site."

"We don't. We get them to evacuate."

"The whole room will panic."

"Here's how," Six said. "You get to the podium and tell the chairman."

"Interrupt? A billion people are watching and listening."

"If an American-looking man runs up to him, it will freak everybody out."

FIFTY-SEVEN

SIX AND REGGIE quietly entered the voting chamber.

"Go," said Six.

Reggie approached the chairman who sat in his wheelchair in front of the assembly, seeming to enjoy the attention fixed on him as long as he kept talking. He had missed the attention and deference he once had when he was a president constantly present in African media.

Six stood in the corner sweeping the room with his eyes. He moved nearer the door between the chamber and the auditorium where the delegates' personal guards waited, and there smelled a whiff of cigar smoke.

Reggie approached Mussa, who recognized her. The delegates shifted in their seats and murmured. Reggie closed her hand over the microphone attached to Mussa's collar and whispered, "Sir, we have received a threat and must evacuate. We will lead you to the bunker where everyone will be safe and the voting can proceed."

The delegates in the audience began stirring uncomfortably.

"Mr. Chairman, the voting must proceed. We can never arrange a second gathering like this one. Things must proceed as planned. The threat is from a known enemy of democracy."

Although droplets of sweat formed on Mussa's forehead, the chairman remained outwardly calm. He composed himself and made the announcement, ending with "Law enforcement is present, and says the situation is probably an empty threat to stop us from doing what we have gathered here to do. But we shall take no chances." Most delegates rose from their seats to be ushered out. When some delegates seemed agitated or resistant, Mussa boomed through the microphone, "Keep your dignity!" The fifty-four dignitaries filed out of the chamber and guards led them to the bunker.

Six bolted the doors to the voting chamber and he and Reggie entered the auditorium, where the hundred or so personal guards had not been sitting but milling in the aisles and talking, some drinking soda and eating bagged snacks, or smoking cigarettes or cigars. Reggie's eyes swept the room for the man wearing glasses. Reggie saw him, and he saw her. She drew her handgun, and aimed.

"Everybody get down! And get out! There is a bomb!"

The man was quick. He drew his gun and fired in her direction. He missed, and ran for the exit and got through. Six and Reggie chased him. He fired two more rounds when they emerged into the hallway, each bullet splintering the doorframe and missing them by inches.

"Let's separate!" Reggie said.

She took the west hall, and Six took the east, weapons in their hands.

———

SIX FOUND Ophélie in the law library. She was shocked when he burst through the door. She drew her gun. Six's was already drawn and aimed.

They squared off, each aiming their gun at the other.

"Don't make me do this," Six said. He laid his finger on the trigger. "Put your gun down."

"I can't go to prison. Either way, I'm already a dead woman."

"That's not for you to decide. We all have to pay for our sins."

"I can't. You don't know these people."

"We can talk about this later. What have they got on you?"

Ophélie's crystal-brown eyes filled with tears. "My family. They have my family. I know where they have my family now. I was going to save them tonight. Then I was cast out. I had done as they asked. They are finished with me. Now they will kill me."

"Who's they?"

"Forces way bigger than you think. There's nothing you can do about it. They will keep coming."

"And I will keep killing them."

"For how long?"

"Until my last breath. You let collaborators into the building. Why sell out both sides?"

"I wanted out, but I didn't know how."

"You could have just disappeared. I looked you up. Online you don't exist."

"You don't understand," she said. "They would've found me. I have a family."

"Did you know how I knew it was you?"

"How?"

"In Tangier, only you, Reggie, and I knew where we would be. I also had my guys check you out, a little. You had a kid, didn't you? They wanted you back, but you didn't want to, so they used your kid as leverage to force you to do their dirty work. They couldn't let an asset like yourself go to waste. You were the best."

"So now you know everything."

"No. But I suspected you were playing both sides. I wanted to find out why."

"Why not just rat me out then?"

"I knew you would lead us to the big guys. Someone in Chris's close circle was passing confidential info to the other side. And I wondered who would most likely benefit from being a double agent. My answer was you."

Tears streamed down Ophélie's face.

"You're the one who advised Chris about the possible attack in Tangier," said Six. "Wondered how you knew about that. Then I remembered seeing you with that same guy in Lyon."

"I didn't have a choice!"

"You are the only one who knew where Reggie and I were staying."

"There are more of them here," she said. "They did not want to leave anything to chance. No room for error. They are going to kill everyone in the building."

"Lead us to the detonator! You may get a

shorter sentence. And you'll get to live to see your family."

"That won't happen. They will come after me. My daughter and I are already dead."

"Do what's right."

Ophélie shook her head.

"Alright. Just put the gun down."

Ophélie's eyes widened. She tightened her grip on her gun.

"Duck!" she yelled, and several bullets cracked. Six dove to the side, twisting and firing in the direction of the library door. A bullet hit his lower back. It hurt like hell, but the bulletproof vest did not let it penetrate. The shooter dove behind the front desk. Six watched Ophélie slump in her chair, one hand against her neck.

The other man peeked over the desk. It was the guy in glasses. Finally!

FIFTY-EIGHT

"FINALLY!" Karim said. "I've heard a lot about you, Six. Let's see what you are made of."

"You have lost. Just give up."

Six glanced at Ophélie, slumped in a chair opposite him and bleeding from the neck.

"Tell me, Six," Karim said. "How does it feel to know that you have been played? Everything you thought you knew was a lie. She played you."

"I know one thing for a fact. I am going to kill you," Six said.

Karim laughed. "I like that. I expect no less. Otherwise, I would be disappointed. You know," he said. "You and I are alike. We kill, we get what we want, because we can. We are apex predators."

"Except my job is to kill people like you!"

"You killed my father! I was going to let your death be easy, but you made a mistake by killing my father. I cannot let that go."

"You bet I killed him," Six said. "He sounded like a little bitch while he was dying."

"I'm going to cut your head off, and parade it as a souvenir!"

"Not if I kill you first."

The two men exchanged insults, then fired back and forth. Six fled into the stacks of books and crouched there. Then Six's gun clicked. He tried its several times. He had emptied the magazine. He searched for a spare magazine on his waist belt. None. *Crap!*

Karim sensed this. He fired several more rounds, inching closer to Six. Six slid under a book rack onto the other side, then deftly climbed to the top of a bookshelf, waited, and jumped down onto Karim. The impact knocked Karim's gun into the books and crashed both men to the floor. Six charged and pummeled Karim into the library bookshelf. The bookshelf toppled and hundreds of law books fell down.

The two tussled, exchanging punches and groans. With Karim on top and Six on the bottom, Karim tried landing some punches, which Six blocked with his arms. Six gripped Karim's left hand, trapped his left leg, and rolled Karim's body onto his left side, and with a foot began pressing Karim's knee sideways. The jiujitsu move was sure to break any man's leg, but not this man's. Karim escaped the leg lock, ending up on top of Six again. He landed a few more punches to Six's sides. Karim placed his hand along Six's jawline, twisting his neck into an awkward position, and elbowed Six on the nose. Pain shot through Six's nose and face. Six fought his way out of the lock and Karim rolled free. They quickly sprang to their feet and squared off again.

Six wiped drops of blood from his nose with the back of his hand. His enemy was good. Karim was a pro. A worthy opponent. He knew Six's moves and knew how to escape the mount. He had done this for a living. He knew how to fight.

Karim smiled, and said, "Is that all you've got?"

Six went in for a punch. Karim anticipated the move. Karim charged forward swinging fists and doing kick combinations with reckless regard. *Doing too much,* Six thought. He could hear Karim's heavy breathing.

Six could have finished him right there and gone to help Ophélie, who was now slumped in her chair and motionless. Six eluded Karim's movements by dodging side to side and under. Six then countered with a jab that caused Karim to recoil and stumble backward. Six knocked him down with a roundhouse kick. Karim quickly sprang up.

Karim retrieved a jackknife hidden on his ankle and flipped it open, point-down, icepick style. They squared off again. Six kept his eyes on Karim's eyes. Karim led with a double kick, followed with an outside-to-inside arched swing, aiming for Six's carotid artery. Six stepped out of range and in one swoop launched an uppercut with his right hand into Karim's chin.

Now Karim was dazed. Six redirected the blade into Karim, just below the diaphragm, severing Karim's abdominal aorta. Karim squeaked. One leg collapsed from under him, then the other.

Six said, "I promised you I was going to kill you. I tend to keep my promises."

Karim gasped, "Well done, my friend. Be careful who you believe. Be careful who you trust, man. It's hard out here. Looks can be deceiving." Karim smiled, then stared blankly into the air, as if welcoming death.

Six rushed to check on Ophélie. She was in shock and struggling to breathe. Six helped her lie flat.

"It's in the cellar below the voting chamber," she told him. "Hurry. You don't have much time."

"Hang on. I'll call an ambulance!"

"Don't bother," Ophélie said. "I can't go to the hospital. I'm already dead. They have my daughter. Promise you will protect her. Her name is Olivia."

"I will."

She handed Six the contacts for her boss. "Take this to the hookah bar down next to the fish market. From Ophélie. Five p.m. tonight. And take this bracelet. And give it to Olivia."

From the gold bracelet dangled a small gold key.

Reggie arrived, limping, while Six was hunched next to Ophélie. Reggie was bruised and bloodied.

"You think we got them all?"

"I think so."

"How did you know it was him?"

"Lin gave me some intel. I had seen him before," Six said. "There were some inconsistencies. I also recognized this guy back at the Safari Club and in Morocco. Ophélie said they have her daughter."

"We can do the unthinkable for those we love," Reggie said.

Six looked back and saw Karim pull himself up and lean against the library's toppled shelf. "It doesn't matter," he smiled, and coughed some blood, showing blood-stained teeth. His white shirt was soaked red. "I'm going to level this place out. Tick-tock, tick-tock!" He managed to exaggerate the statement by waving his index finger side to side. More blood filled his mouth and his face turned pale, and there flickered a hint of fear in the man. He checked his watch.

"No one is leaving here alive," Karim said.

Six told Reggie, "There is a bomb in the gallery below the voting hall. She said it."

The bomb at that moment exploded nearby. Six was knocked over and he and Reggie were blasted by the flames. Six pulled Reggie to the floor as book stacks flew apart and waves of fire missed them by inches.

"Thanks, partner."

"I owed you one. Remember?"

They helped each other up, then staggered towards what had been the basement. The roof crashed down behind them.

CHAPTER
FIFTY-NINE

SIX AND REGGIE found out that the small key was not real gold but electroplated brass, a real key, from a boutique shop at the Century Mall in the Bole area of Addis Ababa. Reggie used her credentials to convince the boutique shop owner to exchange the key for access to the store's safe.

Contents of the safe included four passports from different countries, a roll of U.S. one-hundred-dollar bills, several USB drives, and a journal. Ophélie had kept details and dossiers on everyone she had worked with, including names and contact information of several influential figures in Europe. A detailed memo outlined plans to thwart the African Union declaration. On the USB drives were details about several clandestine operations, voice recordings, maps and phone numbers.

Inside the journal, on the first page, was a printed photograph, cut in half, of a younger Ophélie holding a baby girl. The photo had started to turn yellowish; it was an old photo. The words *I, with Olivia* were written beneath the photo in blue ink. Six and Reggie wondered who had been pictured on its missing half. The next pages in the journal included updates and maps listing locales in cities where Olivia might be. Her tracking had started all the way from Yvoire, France, to Niger, and the last, here, in Addis Ababa. Six and Reggie made sure the safe was empty. Then Reggie bought from the boutique some makeup to cover her bruises, and a sleeveless glitter top. After the mall, Six drove them downtown to the hookah bar.

Six and Reggie had deliberated about what to do with the gold bracelet. They had decided that Reggie should wear it, hoping that whoever they were meeting from the other side hadn't met Ophélie before and did not know what she looked like.

Reggie sighed. "What if they do know what Ophélie looks like?"

"I'll be right across from you," Six said. "And we have the safe contents. That's your leverage. I'm sure that's what Ophélie wanted to trade in exchange for Olivia."

Reggie said, "It is risky, but this is our only shot at infiltrating their camp and rescuing her family unharmed. And nailing down this operation once and for all."

They parked outside the square and walked into the hookah bar separately. There were several people in the bar including a group of four men on one of the lounges.

Reggie sat on a chair making sure her bracelet was visible. The four men looked at her direction. Her heart thudded. She looked away and ordered a glass of wine.

A few minutes later, three of the men walked towards Reggie. One man approached her while the other two towered on either side. He snatched up her hand and studied the bracelet. He nodded to his comrades.

"Do you have the evidence?"

"Yes."

"Give it to us!"

"Not until I see my daughter first."

The man turned aside, punched in a number on his cellphone, and said something on the phone. Then he nodded to his comrades.

"Bring her along! Let's go!"

One of the three men searched and patted Reggie down. The other hookah bar patrons seemed not to care. Satisfied, the man nodded, and motioned Reggie to follow him. They passed beside Six, who was at a side table pretending to drink tea. The men made a beeline for the back of the bar where, outside, an SUV was waiting.

Ten seconds later, Six stood up and exited through the front door.

CHAPTER
SIXTY

THE FOUR MEN drove with Reggie from the hookah bar around the fish market and past its outdoor kitchen to a back alley where they climbed into another black SUV. Six circled the bar and saw the black SUV exit the square. The signal from the tracker on Reggie's earring was live on his phone.

Six rushed to his car and tailed the SUV at a distance. He noticed two other SUVs pull off from the other side of the road and follow the first one.

The SUVs turned off-road into a high-density residential area, its houses mere shacks made of boards and corrugated iron sheets. They sped through the shack settlement. The populated area gave way to a stretch of tent homes and lean-tos.

The SUV stopped in front of a brick fence with a gate of solid iron. The driver honked and a guard inside slid open a viewing portal on the metal gate to check and confirm. Then the iron gate slid open. Reggie was searched again. The man removed Reggie's bracelet and earrings and put them in a plastic receptacle.

"A guest for Karim," one of the men with Reggie said.

Reggie noticed the fear in the man's voice as he said this. She pretended not to notice it.

"Welcome," the guard said.

"Hello," Reggie said.

"Name?"

"Ophélie."

The man wrote the name into the open logbook. "I hope your travel was okay."

"It was okay," she said, smiling impishly, the way she had seen Ophélie do it.

The man smiled, checking her up and down.

"He is expecting you."

The guard led the four men and Reggie through the front porch of the main house. They knocked and a servant opened the door. There was loud rap music playing, and several people in the room— both men and women. The place reeked of mari-juana, cigarettes, and spilled booze. Reggie noticed all the men had holsters with handguns. There were beer cans scattered everywhere. And some were playing cards.

One man sitting in the single recliner looked Reggie up and down and squashed the butt end of his cigarette into an ashtray.

"You have the evidence?"

"Yes."

He motioned with his fingers for Reggie to hand it over.

"I do not have it with me. I need to see my daughter first before I can take you to it."

"Bitch. You came here all the way without the evidence?"

"You think I'm stupid? After I gave you the evidence I knew you would not keep your word. How would I know I'd see my daughter again?"

The man stared Reggie down. Reggie glared back unflinching. The act was working. The man was believing. Some of the eye shadow and mascara she had applied made her eyes look puffy and red. The look made her desperate-mother act believable.

"You're smart. I give you that. But the boss isn't back yet to give permission for you to see your daughter."

Another man laughed. "He is always late."

"Where is my daughter?"

"She is here. Safe. We wait for the boss. Have a sit."

Reggie sat on the chair next to the kitchen table.

"Thank you," she said, removing her jean jacket, leaving herself bare-shouldered.

Several minutes had passed since Reggie's tracker had stopped and would not move. Six feared the worst. He parked his car a few blocks from the signal, and sprinted forward.

There was an armed guard smoking a cigarette outside the gate. Six jumped from the shadows and launched the head of his club straight at the guard's throat, crushing his trachea before the man could let out a sound. He held the slumping guard to the ground and searched him. Footsteps were approaching behind him. Six tiptoed to the corner in the hedge's shadows. The other guard looked around for his comrade. Frustrated, he turned on his walkie-talkie and walked back from the direction he had come. Six pounced and clamped the man in a choke hold before he could speak into the walkie-talkie. Six took the keys from the man's left cargo pocket. He tried several of them and one finally slid into the lock in the gate. Click. Another voice came through the walkie-talkie from another location and got no response. Six had to move fast.

He squeezed through the open gate and saw the guard walking Reggie and the four men to the main house, where they went in. He waited for that guard to emerge and head for the guard shack, then clubbed him. Hardwood and skull collided and the skull cracked. The man stood stunned. He collapsed to the ground.

Six knocked on the door of the main house. A servant opened, cursing. Six pulled his handgun and set the barrel between the flunky's eyes. The man froze in horror. Six burst into the party room, his gun aimed and firing, using the flunky as a shield. Six bullets, and each claimed a victim who did not have time to reach for their handguns or realize what had hit them. Reggie knocked the guy sitting in the recliner cold with a chair to the side of the head.

She smiled at Six and shouted over the music, "Just in time, partner!"

Six smiled back. "That outfit looks—"

"Not right now."

Reggie extracted from a victim one of the pistols and cocked it. The magazine chamber was full. Six picked up another. Reggie moved the sofa, exposing the women crouched behind it. The women trembled.

"Where is the girl?"

One pointed towards the stairs that led to the basement.

"Go. Leave this place," Six told the five women.

Six and Reggie rushed down the stairs, pistols

pointed. Six kicked in one of the doors. There was Olivia. She was sitting balled up on a small bed, shivering. Reggie approached her.

"Your mom sent us to you. To take you from this place to somewhere safe."

Reggie handed her the bracelet. Olivia did not understand English but seemed to understand this. She took the bracelet from Reggie, studied it, then slid it onto her left hand. She slowly loosened and moved to Reggie and hugged her.

"You're safe now!" Reggie said.

Six said admiringly, "You are a natural at this."

Reggie smiled. "Thanks! Let's go!"

Reggie carried Olivia while Six led the way back up the stairs into the living room and kitchen, gun at the ready.

Six picked up the phone that belonged to the man in the recliner, unlocked it with his finger, then called the last number the dead man had dialed. He put the phone on loudspeaker.

He heard the crackling of the receiver. "Tell me you have good news!" a woman said.

"Your guy is dead. He failed."

"Who is this?"

"Someone who is coming after you."

"You are playing with fire."

"Why do you do all these things?" Reggie said.

"Why not?"

"Don't you want peace?"

"Peace, you say. What is peace, what has it ever been but a mere fleeting moment? Much like wanting to be happy. As long as there are haves and have-nots, the powerful and the weak—there will never be peace."

"You're not going to win," Six muttered.

"They will find someone else to take my place."

"Who?"

"Forces much bigger than you can imagine. People don't really want peace and prosperity or they would have it. Someone will take my place."

"I will be seeing you."

"Not if I come to you first."

There was a pause on the other end.

"Very well then. I shall see you when you see me."

The phone call ended.

While Reggie held Olivia and soothed her, Six searched the place and collected evidence from all the phones and electronics he could find. Finished, he poured gasoline from one of the SUVs and set the place ablaze.

CHAPTER
SIXTY-ONE

May 25

THE ATTACK WAS INTERNATIONAL NEWS, but the results of the vote were to be announced the day afterward, and that would be even bigger news. The declaration and the bombing of the AU headquarters had mobilized the whole continent. It was a field day for the local and international media. Millions of views were focused on Addis Ababa. The coming announcement of the declaration was highly publicized across global networks. Major headlines filled the papers and major and minor news networks celebrated the monumental agreement.

Several conspiracy theories circulated. Some pundits claimed that the attack at the AU headquarters was organized by Pan-Africanist leaders to rally and unify the continent against a common enemy and force the declaration to pass, and should it pass, it would be challenged in court.

Some blamed the destruction of AU headquarters on France and the West since they had been doing such things for centuries. Others pinned it on religious extremists. In the wake of the bombing, some pundits speculated on what might happen to those responsible. Regardless, there was an outpouring of support from those who sympathized with the African plight and an increase in anti-Western sentiment across the continent.

The video showed all delegates from all fifty-four African Union member states emerging from the AU headquarters bunker. Some looked shaken; some did not. They were surrounded by thousands of people waiting for the announcement and millions watching online and on TV.

Six and Reggie were watching from their bed-and-breakfast beds, where they stayed all day. At 4:00 p.m., Mr. Mussa, the chairman of the AU Assembly, in a wheelchair, in front of the lineup of delegates gave a powerful unifying speech which some commentators marked as the first State of the Union address for the united continent. Mussa called for one Africa, what he referred to as "a new beginning for the dream our ancestors died for. A dream now realized." He called for unity and peace. He said, "Now we begin a journey that will reveal to the world who we are as Africans, as one people."

The AU delegates had deliberated in the bunker. The declaration passed with a near-consensus vote of forty-eight to six, then was ratified by each member state. They were now the AU Congress.

"Who would've thought this day would come?" Reggie said.

"I didn't. Guess you can never say never."

"The future looks bright. I can't wait for what's next."

A notification beeped on Six's phone. He checked it.

"What is it?" Reggie said.

"Look." Six handed the phone to Reggie.

It was a photo of the first page of Ophélie's journal. The phone showed the cut photograph as it had been when it was whole. What had been cut away was the image of a man. Reggie looked at the photo.

"Ophélie and Olivia! Who is the man? Is that Karim?"

"Ten years ago. He had some nice sideburns back then."

"Where did you get this?"

"It was on one of the USB drives."

"Now we have the complete picture."

The caller relayed a few more details about Ophélie. Then Six told Reggie, "Ophélie and Karim met in France at a bar during training. He was such a gentleman. They fell in love, had a daughter, then one day he decided he had to go back to his father. He had never told the truth about who his father was. According to Ophélie's journal, during a broadcast from a state-run Congolese radio station which Karim liked to listen to all the time, the radio host said: *All hail the chosen! Long live the Eagle!* Karim left them that day, at that moment. She did go back later and listen to the broadcast, wondering what had stirred him and maybe how to get him back. The radio host had repeated that same phrase four times and eventually she figured it out. The repeated phrases were a message for Karim that it was time. But confronting Mubarak and

Karim on their home turf was way out of her league, and anyway, Olivia was more important. Karim had used their daughter as extortion for Ophélie's compliance to help their cause."

Reggie was incredulous.

"He had been groomed his whole life waiting for that moment," said Six.

"How did you know all this?"

"My guys dug it up for me. I had my suspicions," he said. "When Ophélie was shot by the stray bullet meant for me, she was hesitant to fire back. She could have killed Karim at that range. I saw in her eyes that she was pleading with him. When I killed Karim, he told me to be careful whose words I believed, and that looks could be deceiving.

"When I first met her in France, she mentioned she grew up in the South of France. So that narrowed things down. Schools, yearbooks, rolls of registered voters, and so on."

"She loved him."

"I believe so. Even he didn't want to kill her. When he shot her, his emotions were everywhere. That's probably why I was able to kill him. The guy was very good at what he did."

"She went to her grave still loving him."

"And he was torn between obeying his father and love."

"What kind of a man weaponizes their kid for extortion?" Reggie said.

"It happens more than you can imagine."

"This guy couldn't change?"

"That we will never know," Six said.

BACK IN ZIMBABWE, Six and Reggie had a belated British breakfast at the bed and breakfast: toast, margarine, jam, baked beans, sausage, sunny-side-up eggs, and sweet, fatty ground beef. It was all very good.

"Doesn't it feel good to sit and do nothing?" Reggie said.

"It does!" Six said, feeling the bandage on the side of his neck.

Reggie held her teacup with both palms and stared at Six.

"About the next-to-the-last time in Vic Falls," Reggie said.

"What about it?"

"I don't want you to think that I am one of those—"

"I don't. I liked it."

"Thank God."

"But you and I know this might not be the best time to pursue anything more than a kiss."

Reggie remained quiet. After a brief pause, she said, "Why not?"

"Our job. It's unpredictable. I might not be always able to protect you. I care about you. And I can't take that risk. Maybe when time is right, we will settle down. I want to be there for you and my kids."

"Kids, huh?"

"Yes, I like kids. Five at least, if I can."

They laughed.

"Easy to say when you're not the one who will be popping the babies out."

"Fair point. But hey, got to keep the bloodline going."

"I do love kids, though."

"Good work, partner."

"I know. You too."

"You think this declaration will finally be recognized internationally?"

"I hope so. I sure will be glued to my TV tomorrow to see what United Nations will declare."

"Long time coming."

"Got the scars to remember it."

"The forefathers would be proud."

"They sure would. I know they are."

"This is far bigger, more powerful than you and I could ever handle on our own," Reggie said.

"What we did is good for now," Six said.

Then for a time they simply sat and rested, numbing themselves by scrolling through their phones.

A notification dinged on Reggie's phone. She picked it up.

Six snickered. "You have those on?"

"Not always. Today is an exception."

She unlocked and checked the phone.

Reggie said, "The AULEB director's report has been published!"

Reggie handed her phone to Six.

Six scrolled through the headline article. France's foreign affairs minister had been accused of ordering an unauthorized mission, of war crimes, supplying illegal arms to African countries, and inciting violence and civil wars in foreign countries, among other crimes. Her actions were undergoing further investigation and would likely end up in front of the international court.

"She is just a scapegoat," Reggie said.

"Of course someone has to take a fall for it. I think this whole thing goes deep and all the way to the top."

The article also reported that MI6 together with the AULEB had killed the infamous crime lord Asan Mubarak, who had evaded officials for decades, and Mubarak's assets in Switzerland and Malta had been frozen, and the illegal mines would be given to a local mining cooperative. The United Nations was proposing a land reclamation program for the families and villages displaced by Mubarak's operation. And each of the families would receive a sizable amount of money in restitution.

There was more: Several prominent figures had been implicated in the crime web, including the former Victoria Falls mayor, Mayor Hove, who was charged with coordinating a Triple Z smuggling network across Africa and Europe. Based on the information Reggie's team and Six had provided, several of those suspected of involvement with the triple Z trade, and the money laundering, with estimates in the billions, had been extradited by MI6 to Britain, where they would be held awaiting trial by the African Union court. Mayor Hove had been charged by the local Central Investigation Department with running an illegal business behind bars, resulting in endangerment of lives and very possibly would be sentenced to life in prison. Several members of the team of bandits had offered plea deals to testify against the French minister and their boss, Asan Mubarak.

Data collected by AULEB, MI6, and INTERPOL was able to implicate Mubarak on several counts, including leading a terrorist organization, human trafficking, violating human rights, mineral exploitation, and money laundering, with connections to the French minister and a German arms dealer who had been selling ammunition to Mubarak. Most of the artillery confiscated at Mubarak's compound had been German-made and deliberately manufactured and sold without lot numbers and serial numbers.

In an international backlash, there were calls for France's foreign minister to be held accountable and pay reparations to all African nations France had exploited.

Reggie said, "I took the liberty to omit Ophélie and Lin's involvement and other specifics in the final report. And Olivia."

"Thanks."

"Ophélie was just a number to them. She doesn't exist. At least her daughter can live her life freely."

"She is in a good protective custody program. I'm positive she will find a good family."

"Justice always prevails."

"You can't say that."

"It happens in due time. That's how things have always worked since the beginning of time. You can call it karma. Until then, we keep doing what we do best. Putting the bad guys in body bags."

"I have a feeling this is only the beginning."

"It is. But we will be ready when our services are required."

THREE HOURS LATER, they parked their Land Cruiser in front of the hospital.

Six turned to Reggie. "Thanks again for driving me here to see Grandma Grace."

"Of course. I like her."

Six smiled. "That's a dangerous word. Be careful. Grandma falls in love faster than I do."

"What's next after this?"

"Doing what I've always done. Take some time off. Spend a few days here with Grandma Grace. Travel. You?"

"What are you going to do about your dad? After what Chris told you?"

Six looked blankly out the window. "I don't know yet. It's all still unreal to me. Like, I have filed that memory in some hidden corner of my brain. But I know at some point I will want to find out who killed him and my mother."

"You're afraid you won't like the answer."

"What about you?" said Six. "What's next?"

Reggie shrugged. "Have to be back at the office in two days!"

They got out of the Land Cruiser and walked towards the hospital entrance. They knocked at the hospital room door. Grandma Grace smiled. She opened her arms wide. "You! Come on, you two!"

She squeezed them a little too long and they squeezed back.

"Ouch!" she yelped. "Easy on the leg, big guy, my hip is still in a cast."

"Sorry!"

"I'm kidding! I knew you would come back."

Six and Reggie exchanged glances. They laughed.

AUTHOR'S NOTE

I hope you enjoyed 'THE DECLARATION'. As always, if you enjoyed this book, a review would be much appreciated as it helps other readers discover the story.

Sign up at jmanyanga.com to be notified of giveaways, new releases, and updates.

ALSO BY J.M. MANYANGA

The Smoke That Thunders: A Six Thriller

AORATOSIA: Invisible Within

MORE ADVENTURES

The character SIX emerged from observations by the author through travels around the world. J.M. Manyanga believes every person he encounters and every place he visits has a story, and that we can all do better if we are careful enough to look. Follow him on social media for updates on upcoming SIX adventures.